MY BROTHER'S BEST FRIEND

—

LEARNING TO SING LIKE A GIRL

Natasja Eby

Copyright © 2019 Natasja Eby

All rights reserved.

No part of this publication may be reproduced, stored in a retrieval system, or transmitted in any form or by any means, electronic, mechanical, photocopying, recording, or otherwise—except in the case of brief quotations for the purpose of critical articles and reviews—without written permission from the author.

ISBN-13: 978-1072564980

The characters and events portrayed in this book are fictitious. Any similarity to real persons, living or dead, is coincidental and not intended by the author. Should you find yourself inhabiting the body of another person, please seek medical attention immediately.

Cover and book design by Natasja Eby

Published by Natasja Eby
https://natasjaeby.blogspot.com

DEDICATION

For you, dear readers who love body-swapping,
gender-swapping fun.
Enjoy.

ACKNOWLEDGMENTS

Thank you to the following people:

Beth, Cynthia, Eli, Gina, Matt, Michelle, Vicki, and the Instagram #writingcommunity for being 100% supportive.

CHAPTER ONE

"Alright, Jess," Cassidy said, flipping her dark hair over her shoulder. "This is it. This is my summer."

Jessica smiled and listened patiently like the good friend that she was. In truth, she was really just more anxious for Colin—her boyfriend and Cass's brother—to get home. But she couldn't say that; it would be disloyal.

Cass held up a finger. "Got the audition." A second finger. "Now to get the lead in the community musical." A third finger. "And then—get over Ian Stokes."

Jess giggled. "Don't you think that's gonna be a little hard since he'll probably be spending *a lot* of time here?"

"Yeah, but not every day," Cass said, batting her eyelashes at Jess. "Not the days that Colin will be with you. Right?"

Jess smiled, her cheeks turning the softest shade of pink. Cass thought it was cute that even after almost three years of dating, Jess could still blush over the fact. And in general, Jess and Colin were always super cute together.

But that thought just made Cass sad, because she and Ian used to be cute together all the time, too. And now look at them. She couldn't stand to be in the same room as him, couldn't stand what he'd done to her, all while acting like he was totally innocent.

It was just an unfortunate happenstance that Ian was Colin's best friend, which meant that he hung around with Colin a lot.

"Alright, first step in the plan," Jess said, snapping Cass out of her thoughts. "Sing-along musical night."

Cass smiled. At least she could always count on Jess to be there for her, no matter what. When Jess and Colin had first started dating, Cass thought she might have lost her best friend forever. But actually, it had only brought her and Colin closer together as siblings. And she wouldn't change a thing about that.

"I'll go get the popcorn," Cass said, jumping up from the couch. "You get the movie set up."

As Cass waited for the popcorn to pop, she thought about their last few weeks of school. Colin would be graduating soon and he and Jess were going to prom in a couple of weeks. Which meant Ian would be going to prom, and probably dancing with every available girl there. And it didn't bother her. Not at all. Because they were done. It was over between them.

"Oh!" Cass jumped when she realized she could smell burnt popcorn.

She immediately turned the microwave off and opened the bag. Grimacing, she shook it a bit. There were only a few darkened kernels, nothing they couldn't eat around.

"Sorry, it's a bit burnt," she said as she returned to Jess.

Jess smiled kindly. "That's okay. We'll throw those ones at the screen during the annoying parts." Cass gave her a look, so she amended, "And then pick them up as quickly as possible."

Cass giggled. "That's better."

* * *

"Good stuff, Stokes!" Coach called from the sidelines.

Ian smiled to himself. He'd never played better or harder. This summer was going to make or break it for him and so far, it looked like it would make it.

"Col!" Ian called.

Colin, who'd been running up the field with the ball between his feet, didn't even need to look up to know where Ian was. They'd been playing soccer together since they were little. For years, they'd been signed up by the same team because everyone knew that together, they were unbeatable.

Colin passed the ball to Ian with just enough time for Ian to kick hard and score the last goal of their game. His team cheered and he looked over at Colin, pumping his fist in the air. Colin smiled and raised his fist back at him.

"Alright, bring it in, guys!" Coach waited as all his players rushed towards him. When they had all gathered around him, he said, "Next week's game is important. Not only because it's our opener, but there will be a lot of scouts there. For those of you graduating, you could get some good scholarships."

Though he was including all of his players in the statement, he frequently made eye contact with Ian. And Ian knew there just had to be at least one scout there specifically for him. Maybe one for Colin, too. He deserved as good a scholarship as Ian.

"Good hustle today," Coach said. "See you all tomorrow."

Ian and Colin broke away from the group to do some stretches before leaving the field. Colin nodded at Ian's feet.

"You need new shoes," Colin said.

"Yeah," Ian said as he pulled his shoes off. The laces were half ripped, the inner soles had come out long ago, and the seams were beginning to rip apart. "I'll buy some new ones when I make it big, I guess."

Colin chuckled. "I can't let you play in front of those big shots in *those*. Come on, I'll spot you. If we get them today, you'll have lots of time to break them in before the game."

Ian smiled. "Alright, if you're sure, man."

"I'm sure," Colin said easily. "I just need to stop at home first."

Ian sighed and just like that all his good feelings disappeared. If they went home, they would most likely run into Cass, and Cass hated him now for reasons still unknown to him. "Do you have to?" he asked.

"Yes," Colin said, putting on his street shoes.

"Why?" Ian asked. "Gotta freshen up for the sports store or something?"

Colin rolled his eyes. "No, it's just...Jess is there and I want to say hi."

Oh, that gooey voice and those doe eyes. Colin would do anything for Jess, but that didn't mean Ian had to. Then again, he'd do almost anything for Colin, including unwanted interactions with Cass.

"Fine," Ian grit out as they made their way to the parking lot. "For true love, I can suffer through true hate."

"She doesn't hate you," Colin said, cracking open the passenger door of Ian's car. It creaked as it opened, and Colin grimaced.

"Try telling her that," Ian muttered as he tried to get the car started. It only took three times, but finally the engine roared to life.

* * *

Halfway through the movie, Cass heard the front door open and the sounds of Colin's footsteps. Then another pair of feet that she knew could only belong to Ian.

"Ugh," she let out. She paused the movie and waited for the inevitable.

Colin poked his head in and smiled, but not at her. At Jess. "Hey," he said in his smooth voice.

"Hey, babe," Jess said, rising with her arms open.

Cass tried not to roll her eyes. They saw each other almost every day; she didn't see why it should be so important to hug every time one of them walked into the room.

"We're going out," Colin said. "But I just wanted to know—are we still going out to dinner with your parents this weekend?"

"Yup," Jess answered.

"Well, what am I wearing?" he asked a little impatiently.

"Oh." Jess gave Cass an apologetic look. "Do you mind if I go upstairs quickly?"

"No, not at all," Cass lied, waving her hand.

As soon as Jess left the living room, Cass could just feel a pair of eyes boring into the back of her skull. But she refused to acknowledge Ian's presence.

"Hey, Cass," he finally said softly.

She rolled her eyes for no one's benefit and glanced at him out of the corner of her eye. He was leaning against the doorframe, with his stupid muscular arms crossed.

"Hi," she said tersely. "Would you stop staring at me?"

He sighed and stepped a little farther into the room. "I just wish I could see you happy again."

"So, why don't you look for a picture of me that you haven't deleted off your phone and stare at that?" Cass snapped.

He was silent for a moment before saying, "I still have all my pictures of you."

Cass made the mistake of turning to fully look at him. At his deep blue eyes, his magnificently wavy blond hair, his strong jaw line. She swallowed hard. She wished she wasn't so attracted to him still. It wasn't fair, really, that even after a person broke your heart, they could still draw you in like that.

"What do you want, Ian?" she whined.

His eyes narrowed at her tone of voice. He stalked into the living room and plopped down on the couch, entirely too close to her. Her mouth gaped open as he reached into her bowl of popcorn and grabbed the largest handful he could manage.

"I want your popcorn," he said, before shoving almost the whole handful into his mouth.

"You are such a pig!" she shouted in his face.

She went to pull the bowl away from him, but he grabbed the edge and pulled it back to himself. The popcorn jumped around as they played tug of war with the bowl. Normally, that would have annoyed Cass, but she was more irritated with how juvenile Ian was acting. She pulled too hard at one point and Ian let go, causing kernels to go flying out of the bowl and onto the couch and floor.

"Look at what you did!" Cass exclaimed, throwing her hands in the air. "Now there's popcorn all over the place."

Ian stood up and started walking away, making sure to step on as many kernels as he could. With a smirk, he said, "Guess you better get cleaning, then."

"No way," she said, jumping up. "Help me clean this up. You made most of the mess."

He grunted and stooped over to start picking up the popcorn. "Ugh, fine, if you're gonna be like that—"

"Like *not* wanting you to make a mess in my house?" she snipped at him. "Yeah, I'm gonna be like that."

"I *said* I would help out," he said as he dropped some of the kernels back into the bowl.

"You know what? Just forget it," she snapped. "I can do this myself. Go wait for Colin somewhere else."

"No, I'll help you," he said, his voice softening.

"I don't want the help anymore."

Cass bent over to reach for more popcorn. She tried to edge Ian towards the doorway, but instead he reached out for the same spot as her. As she straightened up, her head hit something hard.

"Ouch!" she heard, just before blacking out.

CHAPTER TWO

Ian put a hand up to his head, which felt a lot weirder than it should have. He ran his hands through his hair—*all* the way through a long, silky mane that he'd never had before in his life. The hair ended at the top of a pair of breasts that *definitely* didn't belong on his body.

Finally he opened his eyes and looked down at himself, or rather at Cass's body. He screamed, and the sound that came out was the girliest, most high-pitched sound he'd ever heard. When an accompanying male cry sounded a few feet away from him, he looked up sharply.

There on the ground sat Ian's doppelganger. Ian crawled backwards away from the body as quickly as he could, his eyes wide, his heart racing a million miles a minute.

"Why do you look like me?" his body said, its face drained of any colour.

"Why do you look like *me*?" he countered in Cass's snooty voice.

"...Ian?"

"Cass?"

Cass stood up, slowly and carefully, stretching Ian's body to its full height. "Okay, what is happening? Why are you in my body? I want it back."

Ian started patting down Cass's body, saying, "Take it, please."

"Stop touching it!" she yelled, waving her arms frantically.

Ian dropped his hands immediately, his face flooding with heat. "Sorry," he mumbled. "Okay, what do we do here? How did this even happen?"

She crossed her arms over her chest. "Well, *you* were being an idiot and smacked your head into mine."

"Excuse me?" Ian squeaked out. "You were the one being an idiot. *I* was trying to help you clean up, like you asked me to. You got in the way and now we're stuck in each other's bodies."

Cass scowled, making Ian's lips turn down at a comically low angle. "Stuck? We better not be stuck. Colin and Jess will be down here any minute. So give me my body back."

Ian growled, or at least tried to, but Cass's voice didn't really do that. "Trust me, there's nothing I'd like more than to be as far away as possible from your body. But do you think I have any idea how to do that?"

"I don't think you have very many ideas in your head, no," Cass said, shaking her head with an eye roll.

"Oh, they're coming down," Ian said. He could hear Colin's and Jess's soft footsteps on the stairs.

"I knew it," Cass said, drawing his eyes up to hers. She had a tiny smile on her face. "I knew I had better hearing than you and you didn't believe me."

He rolled his eyes. "Is now really the best time to bring that up?"

The footsteps drew nearer and Cass put a hand up to her lips. "Shh, they're almost here. Come on, let's clean up this mess."

Ian rolled his eyes. He couldn't believe she was still on about that. "And then what?" he whispered.

"We'll figure it out," she whispered back.

"Hey, we're ba—" Colin cut himself off, his hazel eyes growing wide at the sight in the living room. "What happened here?"

"I was being an idiot," Cass said quickly.

"Well, it doesn't help that I'm always such a klutz whenever Ian's around," Ian said, smirking at her.

Cass bit her lip so hard, it almost hurt. Colin looked at her and then Ian with one eyebrow raised high. Then he looked at Jess, who just shrugged with a little amused smile on her face.

"Okay, well...why don't you just get the vacuum, Cass?" he asked, looking straight at Ian.

"Right," Ian said, laughing at himself. "Of course. I'll get the vacuum. The one that we keep..."

"In the front closet," Cass hissed. She smiled to cover up the tone of her words. "I know that, because I spend too much time here."

"Are you guys okay?" Jess asked, shaking her head a bit.

"Yup," Ian said quickly. "Gonna go get that vacuum."

He rushed out of the room and went to the front hall. There, he stopped in front of the mirrored closet doors. There was Cass, with her dark hair, smoky hazel eyes, and perfectly curvy body. He blew a deep breath out through her lovely lips. Maybe if she didn't hate him so much, the situation wouldn't be that bad.

"Don't tell her that," he mumbled to himself.

He grabbed the vacuum and went back to the living room, where Colin and Jess were helping Cass pick up the big chunks of popcorn. He watched her for a minute, leaning over awkwardly in his body. Did she hate him more or less now that she was in there? Who knew?

"Alright, move aside," he said, plugging the vacuum in.

"Cass," Colin said, leaning down to pull the plug back out. "You know that outlet doesn't work."

Ian shrugged as he watched Colin go to another outlet across the room. "Some things are worth giving a second chance."

He glanced at Cass quickly but she just rolled her eyes. His eyes? Hers, for now.

"That's not how outlets work," she said bitterly.

Colin frowned at both of them and then exchanged a curious glance with Jess. "Okay, Ian, can we just go out now?"

Cass swallowed hard. Go out? Where were they even going? "Actually, I need to talk to Cass for a minute. Alone."

Colin sidled up to her and said under his breath, "We talked about this, man."

"It's not about that," Cass whispered back. She could only assume what *that* was, but she knew it definitely wasn't what she wanted to talk to Ian about.

"No, it's fine," Ian said. "We'll go…up to my room."

Cass folded her hands over her chest as her heart started beating faster. "To your room?"

"Yes," he said slowly, nodding his head towards the doorway.

"Right," Cass said. "Okay. Just wait here, okay, Col?"

His eyebrows squished together and he looked between Cass and Ian. Then he shrugged and put his arm around Jess. "I guess a few more minutes wouldn't hurt."

Cass led Ian up to her bedroom and shut the door behind them, grateful that her parents weren't home. They would certainly find it suspicious if she shut herself in her room with her ex, of all people. She faced Ian and crossed her arms.

"What?" he asked, mimicking her pose.

"What did Colin mean that you guys have talked about it?" she asked.

"Talked about what exactly?"

Ian's face went red and he half-turned away from her, shaking his head. He blew out a long breath. "Can we just figure this out, please?"

"What do you want to do, exactly?" she asked.

"We can't keep Col and Jess waiting any longer," Ian said. He shook his head again. "Let's just...pretend to be each other for a few hours, okay? Then tonight we'll try to see if we can...fix this."

Cass stared at him for a moment. "Fine," she finally said. "I guess there's not much else we can do."

She started for the door, but he reached out and took her forearm. "Cass, wait. There's..."

She put her hands up in question and asked, "There's what?"

"There's something else," he said, waving his hands in the air like that would help. "When Colin and I go out, you know...sometimes when there's a pretty girl, one of us will say, like, 'Hey, she's hot.' And the other one usually says, 'Yeah, she is hot.' And that's it. There's nothing more to it, okay?"

Cass looked into her own hazel eyes, trying to figure out what that was all about. Ian's expression was open; he was being serious and not trying to provoke her, but she couldn't help feeling irritated anyway.

"Oh, nothing more than that, eh?" she asked sarcastically.

"It doesn't mean anything," Ian insisted. "It's just...an appreciation."

Cass bit her lip again, hard. After a moment, she said, "So what you're saying is, you want me to go out with my brother and ogle—oh, sorry, *appreciate* all the hot girls we see and I'm guessing I'm not supposed to tell Jess you do that."

His gaze fell to the floor and he nodded wordlessly. "It's just for a day, so he doesn't think anything weird is up, okay?"

"You know what?" Cass said with a smirk. "This'll be easy. I can act like a pig for a day."

Ian looked up sharply. "Cass, come on—"

"You, on the other hand, get to watch a musical with Jess," she said, leveling him with a look. "And you better sing along, otherwise she'll know something's wrong."

He sighed. "Which one is it?"

"*Mamma Mia*," she answered. "The words are on the screen, the melodies are in my heart. And *don't* strain my voice."

"Fine," he spit out. "Don't make me look like a pushover."

"Haven't you been doing a fine job of that already?" she asked.

"You know what?" Ian stomped over to her, annoyed at how much shorter he was than her now. "You'd be way hotter if you knew how to not be so insulting all the time."

Cass lifted an eyebrow, looked her own body up and down, and snorted. "And I've never seen you hotter."

Ian shook his head. "Just get out of here okay? I'll come find you later."

"*Fine.*"

"And be good to my car," he said.

"Whatever," she said, rolling her eyes. What could she possibly want with Ian's old, crappy car?

With their arms crossed and deep scowls on their faces, they went back to Colin and Jess. They were sitting on the couch, kissing, being cute, and totally unaware of anything around them. Cass cleared her throat, making them jump.

"Let's go," she said sullenly, making Ian sound—gasp!—like a pushover.

Colin kissed Jess one more time and jumped up off the couch. Ian sat awkwardly in the spot he'd vacated, wondering how long he'd have to put up with pretending to be Cass.

Jess craned her neck to look out into the hallway and then said in a low voice, "Okay, what did he want?"

"Huh?" Ian said, his face scrunching up.

"I-an," Jess over-enunciated. "What did he want...in your bedroom of all places?"

Ian grunted in a very unladylike way. "He wanted his stupid sweater back. And I still won't give it to him." That much, at least, was the truth. Maybe now he could take it without her knowing.

"Oh, Cass," Jess said in a sympathetically gooey voice. She squeezed Ian's shoulder. "Don't forget about goal number three."

Whatever that was supposed to mean. "Let's just watch the movie, okay?" Ian said weakly.

Throughout the rest of the movie, Ian couldn't quite bring himself to sing along, though he did try a couple of times. Jess, noticing that he wasn't into it, quieted down after a while, and they watched in near silence.

When the movie was over, she turned to him and said, "Seriously, is everything okay? You didn't even sing your favourite part."

"The Winner Takes It All." Ian didn't have to ask to know which song was Cass's favourite. "It's fine," he said.

"Yeah, I know what that's code for," Jess said.

"What?" he asked.

"You know, if Ian's really bothering you, you could just ask Colin to get him to leave you alone," Jess suggested gently.

Ian nearly choked on the advice and struggled to keep his facial expression neutral. Jess obviously didn't know that Colin had already tried that twice and Ian had told him twice that he wasn't completely ready to give up on Cass.

"You think I should?" he squeaked out.

"I mean, if he's really bugging you..." She shrugged, tilting her head to the side to stare at him. "Do you still like him or something?" she asked, not unkindly.

"No, I pretty much hate his guts." That much he could say with certainty.

"Cass..." Jess smiled, her blue eyes lighting up. "You don't have to hate him just because you aren't together anymore."

He looked into Jess's eyes, a little smile playing on his lips. He was glad Cass had a friend like her. "That's a very excellent point."

She laughed out loud. "Okay, I gotta go, girl. See you tomorrow."

"Tomorrow?" he asked as Jess stood up.

Jess' eyebrows drew in. "Yeah. We still have to go to school."

"Right, yeah, of course," Ian said, flicking his hand. "See you in class."

Jess gave him a tight hug, which he had to admit made him feel a bit better. Boys rarely hugged each other for any reason, let alone just saying goodbye. It made him grateful once again to know that Cass had such a nice friend.

Now that he was all alone and had nothing to do, he decided to go back to Cass's room and take back his sweater once and for all. However, once he was in her room he noticed something that he hadn't noticed earlier: it was a mess.

There were clothes strewn everywhere, the bed was unmade with about five thousand pillows all over, and the vanity table was littered with so many makeup products it made Ian's head spin. He lifted up a few pieces of clothing but if he moved too much, Cass would know that he'd gone through her stuff.

With a sigh of frustration, he sat in front of her vanity table. The edges of the mirror were lined with pictures, most of them of Cass and Jess or Cass and Colin. But there was one picture in the right-hand corner that caught his eyes.

He touched it gingerly with his red-tipped fingers. He knew this picture because it was a selfie he'd taken himself this past winter. They'd gone all the way to Nathan Phillips Square in Toronto to go skating and he had stopped to take a picture of them in their winter hats and scarves.

They both looked so happy—they *were* so happy.

"If you hate me so much, what is this picture still doing here?" he asked out loud.

CHAPTER THREE

Cass followed Colin out of the house and then they stood in the driveway together. Colin waited. Cass waited. And then she realized...that was Ian's dumb car in the driveway.

"Anytime, man," Colin said, gesturing to the car. "What, did you leave your keys inside or something?"

"Umm..." Cass felt her front pockets and then...the back ones. There she found the keys. "No, I've got them." She reached into the right back pocket, cursing Ian for having such a toned body. Breathing deeply, she willed her cheeks not to burn so badly.

She unlocked the car and sat in the driver's seat. While Colin got in, she checked the mirrors, pulled her seatbelt on, checked the mirrors again, and finally put the key in the ignition. The engine sputtered as it tried to turn over, so she turned the key back. One more time and finally the car started up.

Alright, Cass, you can do this. You know how to drive. You can do this.

Carefully, she backed out of the driveway, making sure to check all her blind spots. Once on the road, she asked, "Where are we going again?"

"Um, let's try the mall first," Colin said. "We'll probably find something there."

The mall. Okay, she could do that. She could probably drive there blind. Except, obviously she wouldn't do that. She still wanted to get there alive.

"Okay, what did Cass do to you?" Colin asked as they rode along.

Nothing he didn't do to me. "What do you mean?" she asked.

"You're just…acting different," he said. "Driving better, for starters, so I guess I can't complain about that."

Cass smiled, proud that Colin thought she was a better driver than Ian. "I know it's my tendency to wreck everything I hold dear, but I just don't feel like doing that today."

Colin laughed out loud, so hard he actually started coughing. "Whaaat? Okay, I know what this is about. The sweater, right? Do you want me to just steal it back or something?"

"Absolutely not," she nearly shouted, stomping on the brakes at a stop sign. "Cass will give it back when she's good and ready."

He snorted. "Even if she wanted to give it back, it's lost in the abyss of her room and will probably be lost forever."

"Like your room is any better," she snipped.

Colin shrugged and hit the radio's on button. The car started blasting the noisy "music" that Colin and Ian loved so much, but she didn't want to displace her grip on the steering wheel to turn it down.

Getting to the mall wasn't too much of a problem for Cass, thankfully. The problem came when she pulled into the parking lot. Apparently it was a busy day today, and now she would have to park this old thing. Gritting her teeth, she found a spot that didn't look terrible and slowly and carefully pulled in. With an audible sigh, she put the car into park and turned it off.

"Did an old lady take over your body or something?" Colin asked with laughter in his voice.

Cass scoffed without thinking but managed to school her expression in time. "No, I was just being careful. Let's just go in."

They got out and Cass followed Colin, wondering what they had even come to the mall for. As they walked in silence, they passed several girls that Cass considered very pretty, but never pointed any of them out. And neither did Colin, for that matter. So why had Ian gone through a whole explanation over nothing?

Colin led them all the way to the sports store. Of course. The one store Cass was the most unfamiliar with. She stood at the entrance of the store, staring at every foreign and complicated thing in front of her. All her years of shopping expertise wouldn't help her here. When Colin half-turned to her to give her a funny look, she swallowed hard.

"Do you want new cleats or not?" Colin asked.

"Yeah," Cass said slowly. Where the heck was she supposed to find cleats in this place? Oh, Colin was already heading in that direction. He would know. She could just follow him. Right.

She followed Colin over to a section near the back where it felt like there were a hundred cleats on display. They pretty much all looked the same, so she wasn't sure why they needed so many different brands.

Colin sat on a bench nearby and watched her, his eyebrows drawing in more the longer she stood there unmoving. "Get whatever you want," he said. "I know you like the expensive stuff."

Right... At least Cass could look at the prices and figure out which stuff was the expensive stuff. That didn't help with the shoe size, but maybe she could sneakily check the shoes she was already wearing.

She looked up at the wall of cleats, feeling totally lost. They were all. The. Same. And boys thought it was complicated to go shopping for girls. The longer she stood there, the more anxious she started to feel.

"Are you okay?" Colin's voice came from right next to her, making her almost jump.

"I'm just not feeling quite myself today," she whispered. That much, at least, was true.

Colin looked at her in concern, a little thoughtful frown on his face. "Okay...I don't know what's up with you, but I'm going to pick up a pair and buy them. Then we'll take them on the field."

"On the field?" she squawked awkwardly in Ian's low voice.

Colin's eyes widened. "Yeah...that's where they belong." He rolled his eyes and shook his head. He went over the shelves full of boxes, looked for approximately two and half seconds, and then pulled a box out. "Eleven, right?"

"Sure," Cass said uncertainly.

Colin raised an eyebrow and shook his head again. He started towards the checkout and she followed him dumbly. He was quiet while they waited in line, which suited her just fine. She didn't know what he and Ian talked about while she wasn't around and she wasn't sure how to act like Ian without being tempted to just act like an idiot.

The cashier, a pretty girl with short dark hair, smiled brightly at Colin and then turned her attention to Cass. Cass blushed under the attention, which just made the girl's smile grow wider. *Curse Ian and his stupid, adorable face.*

Colin paid and took the box with him. Once they'd left the store, he grinned at her. "That girl was into you."

"Yeah, she was...pretty cute," Cass said honestly. It felt weird though, to admit that a girl who seemed like she was into her ex was cute.

"Cute?" He said, his face scrunching up. "She was hot. Here."

He held the box out to her. She stared down at it, wondering what she was supposed to do with them.

"Come on," he said, shaking the box a bit. "I'm not going to buy them for you *and* carry them."

"Oh!" Cass said. She took the box from him. Colin had bought the shoes for Ian? Why? "Th-thanks."

Colin shrugged. "Whatever. You're *not* playing that game in those old things, alright?"

Cass smiled. She knew that tone of voice. Colin might have been trying to sound gruff but underneath that, he was still just a soft-hearted boy. "You're a good friend, Col."

He smiled and kind of half-rolled his eyes. "Yeah, you, too. Don't make it weird. So, we gonna go break those in?"

Ah, that's what he'd meant earlier when he'd said they would take them to the field. Cass wasn't quite ready for that, though. "Actually, I'm not feeling that great. I'll just take you home, okay?"

"Alright," he said.

Once again, Cass drove as carefully as she could, grateful that Colin wasn't trying to make conversation with her. She had to admit—even though Ian's car was kind of a mess, it was nice being able to drive. By herself. Without someone telling her how to do it.

She pulled into her driveway and almost turned the car off to go inside. But then she remembered she was in Ian's body and if she were really Ian, there was no way he'd go back inside to face her. The thought kind of made her sad, and only made her sadder to realize she'd have to go back to Ian's house.

"Thanks for the shoes," she said as Colin opened the door.

"Yeah, just add it to your tab," he said. "See you later, man."

"See you."

She watched Colin enter the house. Now she'd have to go to Ian's house and pretend to be him until they could figure out how to switch back later tonight. She blew a deep breath out. At least Ian's house was another place could probably drive to blind if she had to.

One more deep breath and she pulled out of the driveway. Ian's house wasn't far but in truth, she kind of enjoyed the drive. Even when the car lurched a bit at a stop sign. And thankfully, no one was home when she got to his house, which meant she could try a little less hard to be like him.

She took the cleats Colin had bought up to Ian's room. She'd almost forgotten how neat he kept his room. Sure, there were a few pieces of clothing that hadn't quite reached the laundry basket and there were two cups half-filled with water on his night table. But other than that, it was pretty orderly in there.

She sat on his bed, put her head in her hands, and cried. It felt good to relieve some of the tension, but it was short lived when she felt Ian's phone ringing in her pocket. She quickly got it out while wiping her tears away with the other hand. Her name was on the call display.

"Hi," she said, trying to make it sound like she wasn't just crying.

"How's my baby?" he asked. Her voice made the question sound a lot nicer, gentler than it actually was.

At first, she thought he was talking about her but that didn't make any sense. And then she realized... "I crashed it. Wrapped it right around a tree. Maybe now you can buy a better one."

"Very funny," he said bitterly.

Cass sniffled. "Do you have any idea what we're supposed to do now? I really don't want to be you anymore."

There was a moment of silence on the line after which he asked, "Are you crying?"

"Ian," she snapped at him, brushing away tears he couldn't even see. "How do we fix this?"

"I don't know, Cass," he said, sounding more desperate than annoyed, even though she could hear a little of that, too. "Let's meet tonight at like...midnight, I guess."

"Okay, where?" she asked.

"My place."

"Which place do you consider your place?" she asked.

"*Mine*—my house," he huffed. "The one where you're currently inhabiting my body."

Cass bit back a snarky retort. "Okay, so...you're going to sneak out at midnight...to go to your ex-boyfriend's house?"

Ian let out a humorless laugh. "Would you rather have your ex-boyfriend sneak into your bedroom tonight? Isn't Colin kind of a...light sleeper?"

As annoying as he was, he had a good point. Neither one of those was a great option. "What about...that park by your house?" she asked.

"Fine," he said. "I'll see you at midnight." Then he was gone without even saying goodbye.

She stared at the phone in her hand. The background picture was a picture of her. The sun was shining on her, making her hair look brighter than it was. But it was her smile that killed her. Right now, she couldn't remember ever being that happy with him and it made her want to chuck the phone across the room.

Instead, she opened up his photo album. The most recent photos were dumb things, like his car and food he obviously thought looked appetizing. But after scrolling a bit, she saw that he wasn't lying about having kept all his pictures of her. He even had pictures that she didn't realize he'd taken.

Fresh tears fell when her eyes landed on a picture of them kissing in front of a famous statue downtown. Everyone took a picture like this, because the statue featured a nameless couple kissing. At the time, she'd found it kind of sweet that he wanted one, too. Now it just made her feel sick.

Ugh. She shoved the phone in her pocket and wiped away her tears. She had to figure this out. There was no way she was getting stuck in this body forever.

CHAPTER FOUR

Pretending to be Cass for one evening meal wasn't really all that difficult for Ian. In fact, he felt quite comfortable in Cass and Colin's home, pretending that he belonged to Mr. and Mrs. Jacobs. The only hitch came when Mrs. Jacobs asked if he wasn't going to practice tonight.

Practice what—well, that should have been obvious to him. But it still took him a moment to realize she meant practice Cass's music. And that might have been fine, except he didn't know how to do music.

"Umm." He hesitated, coughing a little on an appropriate lie. "I don't feel too good tonight, actually. I think I might just go lie down."

"Oh," Mrs. Jacobs said, her eyebrows drawing in in motherly concern. She put her hand against Ian's head. "You don't feel too warm. What's wrong?"

Ian cleared his throat. "Just a little tickle, I guess."

"A *tickle?*" Mrs. Jacobs' eyebrows rose up her forehead, her eyes wide. "Oh dear, no. You go up to your bed and I'll bring you some of your warm water."

Ian furrowed his eyebrows and said slowly, "Okay..."

Not wanting to draw too much attention to himself or tip anyone off, he went straight up to Cass's bed and, with only the slightest hint of misgiving, got in between the sheets. He didn't even bother to change because, well, hopefully it wouldn't come to that. Cass would be livid if he showed up to meet her tonight in something she hadn't put on her own body.

Mrs. Jacobs came up a minute later, a cup on a saucer in her hands. "Here you go, sweetheart. We've got to take care of that voice of yours."

Ian sat up and took the proffered cup. "Thanks," he murmured.

He took a long swig only to find out that was not warm water in the cup. It was some vile combination of foreign spices—he thought, anyway—and it went down horribly. He started sputtering, nearly tipping the liquid over into his lap, but managed to keep the cup upright.

"Oh, honey, are you okay?" Mrs. Jacobs asked, patting him lightly on the shoulder.

"What *is* that?" he finally squeezed out after he was done coughing.

Mrs. Jacobs gave a little shake of her head. "It's your favourite. Lemon and honey."

"Oh." That was lemon and honey? That was a horrible combination. Cass actually drank that? "Oh, right. Sorry. Yeah. I l-love it." He drank some more, trying not to immediately spit it back out.

She reached out and stroked his hair away from his face. "Are you okay? You've been awfully quiet tonight."

Cass *did* have a habit of being overly chatty, but Ian wasn't sure how to be chatty Cass right now. "Yeah, I'm fine mis—*mom*. Mom. I think I just need some rest."

She frowned in concern and patted Ian's head one more time. "Alright, if you're sure. Wouldn't want you to get sick before your big audition."

Ian smiled tightly. "Of course not."

Cass had a big audition coming up? Why hadn't she told him? Oh right, because she wasn't currently talking to him about anything. Well, that would just have to change tonight, wouldn't it?

Ian lay awake in Cass's bed, waiting until he heard Mr. and Mrs. Jacobs go to bed and then Colin. As tempting as it was to go through Cass's phone, he didn't know if he could bring himself to do it. He wasn't sure he wanted to know how much of himself she'd deleted from her life.

Finally, when he couldn't wait any longer, he got up quietly and started heading down the stairs. Lucky for him, he knew where the squeaky spots were so he avoided those easily. Once outside the house, he started sprinting for the park by his house but quickly discovered that Cass's body was not refined for running.

After a few minutes, he gave up and started walking. It frustrated him, to say the least, that he couldn't even make the run from Cass's house to that park. In his own body, that would have hardly winded him, but now he was already breathing heavily.

When he got to the park, he hid behind a bush to make sure there was no one else there. But in fact, there was one lone, long figure sitting in a swing, swiping at his reddened cheeks and sniffling.

Ian came out from behind the bush and cleared his throat to announce his presence. "I can't believe I actually fit in that swing."

Cass looked up, quickly wiping off more tears with the heel of her hand. "You don't really. It's pretty squishy."

He crouched in front of her, discovered that was far too low to the ground, and stood back up. He reached out and put his hand on his own shoulder, shaking gently.

"Don't cry, Cass," he said, trying to sound gentle and not annoyed. "We'll figure this out."

"How?" she asked, rising from the swing. "We don't even know how this happened."

"I don't know." Ian watched Cass pace back and forth in the wood chips covering the playground, her head down. "Maybe we need to..."

"Need to what?" she asked, still pacing.

"Need to..." An idea occurred to him, but she probably wouldn't like it. "Maybe this is about us."

"*Us?*" She stopped pacing to look at him. "What us?"

He took a step closer. "You and me. Maybe it's about us. Maybe we should try—" he tried not to cringe "—kissing."

"Kissing." No, she definitely wasn't happy if the tone of her voice was any indication.

"Or something," he quickly amended.

A muscle ticked in Cass's jaw and he knew what that look on his own face meant. She didn't like the idea one bit. "You would take any opportunity to kiss yourself, wouldn't you?"

"What?" He scrunched up his face. It hadn't really even crossed his mind that that was how it would play out. "No. I'm being serious, Cass. Kissing myself is the last thing on my mind. I just want to be back in my body."

Her jaw relaxed but he could tell she still didn't want to kiss him at all. "There's gotta be something else..."

"Like what?" When Cass didn't answer, he chanced taking one step closer. In a soft voice he said, "Do you really hate me so much you won't even consider trying it?"

Cass looked at him sharply, a little frown between her eyebrows. "I don't hate you," she said, but it came out all huffy and not entirely convincing.

"Okay, so...?" He hated how feeble and insecure he sounded with Cass's voice. *She* didn't normally sound like this, so why did he?

She wiped her hands on her pant legs and gave a little nod. "Okay. Let's try it."

Neither of them moved. They'd kissed thousands of times before; one more shouldn't be that big a deal. But now, like this, and almost five months after they'd broken up?

After what felt like an eternity, Ian finally made the first move. He grabbed Cass's face—*his* face with both of his hands and pulled her close. It wasn't horrible. It was weird sure, but actually, now that she was kissing him back and her arms were around him, and...wait. Cass actually seemed kind of into it.

When he realized that all they were doing was kissing and not returning to their own bodies, he pulled back. She stared at him for a moment, before dropping her arms violently and practically jumping back.

"Well, that didn't work," she said, crossing her arms. She couldn't quite meet his eyes.

"At least now I know I'm a really good kisser," he said, trying for levity since being serious wasn't working out.

She scoffed and finally looked into his eyes. "I was the one using the equipment, not you."

"Yeah?" He smirked. "And how are you enjoying my equipment?"

Cass's face burned bright red, even in the darkness of the night. "Can you *please* try to be serious?"

"What do you want from me?" he said, putting his hands up in surrender. "I don't know how to fix this any more than you do."

"Okay, that's it." She put her hands up in the air. "I'm just going to bang my head against yours."

Ian's eyes widened and he put his hands against her chest to hold her back. "Cass, no."

"Well, that's what got us into this mess in the first place," she said. "Isn't it worth a try?"

He shook his head. "Look, *I* can handle that, but your pretty little head can't. If a kiss didn't work, I doubt a headbutt would. You'll just hurt yourself."

The lines around her eyes softened. "You still think I'm pretty?" she asked quietly.

His closed his eyes briefly, breathing deeply through his nose. "It's not like you stopped being pretty after you broke up with me. You should consider working out, though."

Her mouth gaped open. "Do you think I'm fat?" She looked Ian up and down, checking out her own body.

He looked down, too, a deep frown on his face. Cass wasn't stick-thin; she had curves in all the right places and she knew how to dress them. "Of course not!" he practically shouted, as if that would be more convincing than just stating it. "But working out would give you a little more energy and then I wouldn't have felt like keeling over just from the little jog over here."

"I can't believe you think I'm fat..." she said slowly, quietly.

"You're not fat, Cass. You're—" *Perfect*. He stopped himself from blurting that out. Even if she would believe him, she wouldn't want to hear it from him anyway. "You're getting distracted. What should we do about this?"

She shook her head, chewing on her lip. "Maybe...it'll just resolve on its own."

"What'll resolve?" he asked.

"This—" she pointed back and forth between them "—problem we're having. Maybe it's like a...twenty-four hour..."

"Flu?" he filled in.

That got a little smile out of her. "Maybe something like that?"

"So, what?" he asked. "Just pretend to be each other for a while? Go to school and act like we're not trapped inside someone else's body?"

She nodded, a little cringe on her face. "It couldn't be that bad, right? Just one day? We—we know each other pretty well, right?"

"Right."

Oh, that much was true. Ian knew Cass almost as well as he knew Colin—or even himself. Did Cass still feel that way? Did she think she knew Ian well enough to be him?

"Okay, so...we'll just go to school tomorrow," she said, "and then...wait for the timer to expire."

He nodded and they just stared at each other.

At once, they both said, "Don't dress me in anything stupid."

She laughed. "Agreed."

"Same," he said. "I'll see you tomorrow?"

She nodded. "We'll meet after school, okay?"

"Text me your schedule," he said, getting her phone out of his pocket. "And I'll text you mine."

"That makes sense," she said.

She stared at her phone in his hand and got out his. "I guess...we shouldn't really trade these."

He pursed his lips. "No. Let's just keep each other's. I didn't go through your stuff though, okay?"

"I—" She faltered. "I kind of looked at your pictures."

"Oh."

A little smile appeared on her face. "I didn't delete any of them or anything. I was just...curious. I guess I wouldn't blame you for doing the same."

He nodded. She'd basically given him permission to look through her phone now, but he still wasn't sure if he wanted to. "Okay...I'll see you tomorrow, Cass. Get some good sleep, you're going running with Colin at six-thirty."

She nodded. "Oh, I know. Because I get up before him to do my vocal exercises, which you're going to do. And yes, he *still* makes fun of them, so enjoy that."

"Okay," Ian said. He knew there was no way he was going to do that. He had no idea what her vocal exercises were like and he didn't want to try to figure it out. But being agreeable in this circumstance was better than starting up a new argument.

CHAPTER FIVE

Cass woke with a start and nearly jumped out of her skin. That is—she nearly jumped out of Ian's skin. Waking up in his room was bad enough, but remembering that she was in his body was only slightly worse. She rubbed her eyes and then looked again. Yup. Still his room. Still his body.

The incessant buzzing that had woken her was coming from Ian's phone. She liked to wake up to classical music, but apparently that was too refined for Ian's tastes. Ugh, and now she had to go running with Colin before school. What she wouldn't give for a set of working vocal pipes.

She tried one simple exercise, a glissando that should go from the bottom of her range to the top. But Ian had basically no range and she couldn't place where the notes came from or where they should go, so her voice came out sounding awful.

So that was that, then. There was little of Cass here, just the essence of her very being trapped inside a body that couldn't do any of the things that she could do. Great.

After debating whether she really would get up to go running, the thing that finally got her out of bed was the need to relieve herself—or rather, Ian's bladder. Deciding not to think too hard about it, she went into the bathroom and...aimed carefully. With that out of the way, she considered the shower and then shook her head at herself. She was still hopeful they would switch back at some point today.

She went back to Ian's room and looked into the drawers. "Don't wear something stupid... Well, if you owned anything that wasn't stupid, that would probably help here."

It didn't matter though. She knew what Ian wore and for every occasion. Running with Colin was easy. Shorts and a t-shirt. With only five minutes before she was supposed to meet Colin, she tugged Ian's shoes on and left the house.

Though she wasn't exactly athletic—that much Ian was right about—she found that running wasn't really that bad. At least not in Ian's body. As she ran, she could feel every muscle in his body moving and it was interesting, to say the least. Actually, she kind of liked the way it felt to get her heart racing, to feel the warm wind against her face.

When she got to her house, Colin was just coming out, still tugging on one of his sneakers. Colin waved as she slowed down.

"Sorry," Colin murmured. "I'm ready."

He started running without even waiting for her, so Cass started up again, even though she was starting to feel tired. But Colin kept an easy pace, slower than Cass had. She let him take the lead through their shared neighbourhoods until they looped back around to Ian's house.

"Alright, hurry up," Colin said, pointing at Ian's door. "We're almost late for school."

"Right." Cass nodded and went into Ian's house. For what, she didn't know. Oh! Of course, Ian needed his backpack and...his car keys. Maybe this wouldn't be so bad.

After another careful drive, Cass and Colin made it to school. Colin kept up a one-sided conversation while Cass was still trying to decide what she was supposed to say and how she was supposed to act around Ian's friends. Sure, she'd had a lot of interaction with them, but only as herself. She had no idea what they were like when she wasn't around.

Everyone greeted her like she truly was Ian and all she had to do was nod back at them. That was it. One little head nod and they didn't suspect a single thing.

Colin elbowed her as they walked along the hallway. "There's Christy," he said under his breath.

Cass looked up. There was Christy, a tall, redheaded girl, quietly gathering things from her locker. "So?" she whispered back.

"So?" Colin lifted an eyebrow at her. "She's all alone, go ask her."

As they drew closer, Cass wondered what she was supposed to ask Christy. Was—was Ian planning on asking Christy out on a date? Well, there was no way she'd do that. In Cass's opinion, Christy would thank her if she knew.

With a little shake of her head, she scooted past Christy just as a couple of her friends were joining her.

"Hey, Ian," Christy called just when Cass thought she was safe.

Cass smiled and waved and the smile Christy gave her back made her cheeks go bright red. Colin rolled his eyes, but waited until they'd turned the corner before punching her shoulder.

"What's wrong with you?" he asked. "That was the perfect opportunity."

"Now's not the time," she said, which was the truth anyway.

"Wow, that's a new excuse," he said, stopping outside of a classroom door. "Why you don't you just admit you're not over Cass?"

Cass sighed and looked down at her shoes. There was no answer she could give that would be appropriate, truthful, or in any way fair to Ian.

"Alright," Colin murmured. "I'll see you later." He patted her on the shoulder and then went into his class.

Cass was tempted to just skip Ian's classes—especially since the first one was calculus—but she'd made a deal with him. Pretend to be him, just for the day. And then...and then...

And then what, Cass?

* * *

From the moment Ian woke up, he was disoriented and confused. He had been banking on waking up in his own body. But no, it was Cass's messy room that he saw as soon as his eyes opened.

He could hear Colin getting ready in his room, so he got up like Cass asked him to. He left Cass's room, heading towards the bathroom, but Colin whipped past him, almost knocking him over.

"Hey!" he whined.

"Sorry," Colin threw over his shoulder. "You were supposed to wake me up and now I'm late!"

"I was?" Ian asked. Cass hadn't mentioned anything like that.

Colin gave him a tired glare. "Yeah, with your awful caterwauling. What's wrong with you anyway, you getting sick?"

Ian wanted to snort at the insult, but he knew that Cass would not have laughed. In fact, she'd probably make some disgusted grunt and then try to hit Colin. On the other hand, Ian could hear the note of concern in Colin's voice when he asked if Cass was getting sick, and it was kind of nice, insults aside.

Ian shook his head. "No. Just tired."

Colin stood in the doorway of the bathroom, giving him one last weird look. "Too tired for caterwauling?"

"Yes," Ian snipped and *now* he felt more like Cass.

Colin frowned, shrugged, and then slammed the bathroom door in Ian's face.

Ian went back to Cass's room and looked around. Dressing her body might not have been so bad if there weren't clothes *everywhere*. Finally, after sifting through them, he picked up a clean-looking pair of jeans and a shirt that he knew looked good on Cass. And, of course, a bra. There were only about ten of them lying around, so picking one wasn't hard.

No, the difficulty came when he tried to put it on. Getting it off last night hadn't been a problem, but getting it on was way harder than it looked. He had his arms through the straps and the cups were in place, but every time he tried to hook it up at the back, everything moved and the latch wouldn't catch.

"This is impossible!" Ian shouted to no one. "How do girls do this every day?"

Finally, after some twisting and finagling, he managed to hook the latch. He hoped Cass was right about them switching back at some point today, because he did not want to have to do this for the rest of his life.

Once he was dressed and could hear Colin leaving for the day, he looked briefly at Cass's reflection in the vanity mirror in her room. Her makeup—that he'd neglected to remove last night—was a mess and considering the millions of products sitting out in front of him, there was no way he'd be able to fix it.

"Not today," he said, grabbing the package of makeup remover wipes. He scrubbed at Cass's face until all the makeup was gone and then smiled at his reflection. "Now you look beautiful."

With some time before he had to leave for school, he went down to Cass's piano in the living room. There on the stand were some different songbooks and some loose sheets of music. The pages were covered in little dots and sticks on lines. Of course he'd seen written music before, but he didn't have the know-how or patience to figure it out right now.

Sing her vocal exercises?

"Also not today," he muttered to the piano.

At school, things didn't get any less complicated or confusing for him. Reading girls was like trying to read music—apparently Ian wasn't very good at either. Cass's friends greeted him with hugs and strange looks, making him wonder if he'd dressed incorrectly or if he was missing something else.

Finally, he saw Jess, a welcome face in his mind. At least he knew Jess well enough to feel somewhat comfortable around her.

"Hey, Cass," she greeted him, peering curiously into his eyes. "We're still going shopping after school, right?"

"Yeah, of course," he said quickly. That should be easy enough.

"Great," Jess said, her blue eyes sparkling. "I really don't want to miss that sale on bras."

Inwardly, Ian groaned over his terrible luck. Shopping for anything but bras would have been acceptable. Outwardly, he tried to smile. "Yeah, that would suck."

Jess' eyebrows drew in. "Are you okay?"

"Yeah, why wouldn't I be?" he said with a little shrug.

"You just seem different today," she commented, her head tilted at an angle.

Ian was saved from having to answer by the first bell. He smiled at her. "See you later."

* * *

Getting through Ian's classes was, quite frankly, torture. Cass had none of the prerequisites for learning all of the things that Ian was supposed to be. Who knew he was taking advanced calculus, biology, *and* French? Since when was he interested in any of that stuff? She'd thought that all he liked to do was gym class and sports.

Of course, the sports were no easier for her. She knew how soccer worked—Colin had been playing long enough for her to figure out at least the basics. But she'd had no idea soccer players wore so much clothing. The socks, shin guards, elbow and knee pads, chest protector, shorts, t-shirt.

And then there was the cup.

Oh the cup, which Cass would have done anything to avoid having to put on. But she knew if she didn't put it on, it could be bad news for her *and* Ian. Everything else felt like it was in the right place, but that stupid cup just didn't seem to sit well at all. Cass looked in the mirror in the locker room, trying to see if it was noticeable, but she couldn't even see it. She could only just...feel it.

"You done staring at yourself?" Colin called from the doorway of the locker room. "Let's go."

"I'm coming," she said hastily.

She followed him outside and waited for him to start doing some stretches and warm-ups so that she could copy them. But when the coach called her over to her position—an invisible spot on the field, if you asked her—she feigned not feeling well and asked to sit out for a bit. The coach gave her a funny look, but agreed, though the frown on his face showed his disapproval. Hopefully that wouldn't come back to haunt her later.

* * *

When school ended, Jess found Ian at Cass's locker and waited for him to...do something. Oh right! Shopping. *Great...*

"Come on, the bus won't wait forever," Jess said.

She was still smiling, but was bouncing a little impatiently, so Ian didn't even bother opening Cass's locker. "Ugh, the bus," he accidentally let slip. He hadn't taken the bus since he got his car.

"Yeah, well," Jess said as they started walking, "maybe once we have our full licenses. Or maybe if one of us was dating a guy with a car..."

Ian nearly choked over the words. Was Jess trying to get Cass to go back to him? "Jess..." he said.

"Oh no! I didn't mean Ian," Jess said hastily. "Forget I said that, that was dumb."

Ian shook his head and stayed silent as they travelled to the mall. Jess didn't seem to notice as she kept a one-sided conversation going. At the mall, she led them to one of those fancy lingerie stores that Ian wouldn't be caught dead in...unless he were in a girl's body, that is.

Jess practically tore through the store, picking up at least five different bras, and even handing a couple to him. "Okay, let's go get a change room," Jess finally said, heading towards the back.

A change room? A single one? As in—sharing a change room? Surely Jess didn't mean that... But then she went into one and held the door open for him to go in, too. Now what was he supposed to do?

Jess waved her hand impatiently at him, so he went in and closed the door behind him. Jess lifted off her shirt in one smooth, quick motion and Ian immediately dropped his gaze to the floor.

"Maybe I'll go get my own room," he whispered to his feet.

"Don't be ridiculous. We're saving space this way."

He heard the unmistakable sound of a clasp unhooking and then saw Jess's bra drop to the floor.

"Are you going to try on anything?" Jess asked.

Ian made the mistake of looking up at her, forcing his eyes to go up to hers. Then he watched as she did up the hook of the bra she was holding in front of her. Once it was latched, she turned the bra around, slid the straps on, then pulled everything into place.

He couldn't help the little "huh" that escaped his lips. So *that* was how it was done.

"What?" Jess asked.

"It looks very nice on you," Ian said truthfully.

The deep mauve was a sharp contrast to Jess's porcelain white skin and had all the right amounts of lace. But the longer Ian looked at it, the guiltier he felt. This was his best friend's girlfriend.

"I'm gonna go wait for you out there," he said, turning swiftly to open the door.

"You don't want anything?" Jess asked.

"Nope."

At least, there *was* something he wanted, just not that. He wanted his body back.

CHAPTER SIX

Ian and Cass sat in Cass's living room, watching as the clock ticked by. When they reached the minute that they were pretty sure they had switched bodies 24 hours ago, they held their breaths…and let them back out disappointedly as the clock moved but they didn't.

"Well," Ian said. "This is officially a disaster."

"Tell me about it," Cass said. She couldn't even be offended by the statement because she felt the same way. "What now?"

"I wish I knew," Ian said, slumping down on the couch. "Are we just supposed to…keep pretending to be each other? I can't do that."

"Oh, like it's so hard for you," she said, glaring down at him. "I don't understand any of the things that are happening in your classes. I can't play soccer. I don't know how to relate to your friends."

"*My* friends?" he countered, raising his eyebrows up to his hairline. "Like your friends are any better."

"What's wrong with my friends?" she asked, curious and annoyed at the same time.

Ian sat up straighter and said, "Everything girls say has at least ten different meanings. Like, for example, today all your friends were like, 'Wow, Cass, you're *so* brave for not wearing makeup today.' But like, they don't really mean that."

Cass shrugged. "It kind of is brave to go to school without makeup on."

Ian's eyes grew wide and he pointed a finger at her. "Aha! See? You don't mean that. What you really mean is, 'Ian, you idiot, why did you not put makeup on me?' And the answer, by the way, is that don't know how. So, don't even start with that."

Cass scowled. "You are so infuriating, you know that? You're right, it is easier being you because all I have to do is be dumb all the time and no one notices the difference."

"Well, all I have to do is flip my hair and sing some little ditty and everyone's all over me," Ian said. He punctuated his statement with a poorly executed arpeggio that made Cass cringe to her core.

"That's it," Cass said, grabbing him by the arms. "We're knocking our heads together!"

"Be my guest," Ian shot back, daring her to hurt her own body like that.

A slamming sound was heard through the house before Cass could even make a decision and she abruptly let go of Ian. "Was that the front door?'"

"It's Colin," he hissed as voices wafted over to them.

"And Jess," she added. "They can't find us here like this."

"Let's just...pretend we were making out or something," he said, leaning towards her.

"No way," she said, putting a hand on his forehead to stall him. "That's way less believable than what's actually going on here."

He gave her a withering look but they didn't have any more time to decide before Colin entered the room. As soon as he saw them—with Cass still pushing on Ian's forehead and Ian leaning in at a suspicious angle—he crossed his arms with a scowl.

"What's going on here?" Colin demanded, his eyes sparking with some unnamed emotion.

"Nothing!" they both said, hastily moving away from each other.

Jess came into the room behind Colin and lifted an eyebrow at Ian, obviously thinking that he was Cass. Ian shrugged uncomfortably, but Cass crossed her arms and pursed her lips defiantly.

"What is this?" Jess asked. She looked a little more amused than Colin did.

"It's nothing, Jess," Cass said, waving her hand at her. "I should really go. Just forget I was even here."

She started to leave the room but Colin's hand shot out and gripped her upper arm hard. She frowned down at it and then at him.

"Look, you're my best friend," Colin said, and his face was still twisted into discontent, "but I won't be happy if I found out you came here just to bug Cass."

Cass's chest warmed from the inside out. She couldn't believe Colin was standing up for her to his oldest and best friend, and it made her smile in what she was sure was a silly way.

"I'm not bugging her," she said, glancing at Ian quickly. "But I will go."

"No, don't," Ian said in a defeated tone. "We need help."

Cass forced a laugh and flashed her eyes at him. "No, no, we don't. We're perfectly fine."

"Are you guys trying to work things out?" Jess asked gently. She nudged Colin. "I told you, Cass has been acting weird all day."

Cass shook her head, putting her hand up. "No, we're not. There's nothing wrong."

"Yeah, Ian's been super weird, too," Colin said, narrowing his eyes at Cass. "Spill. What's going on?"

"Nothing," Cass insisted.

"We switched bodies!" Ian exclaimed, jumping up from the couch. "We switched and now we can't get back."

The room fell silent. Cass narrowed her eyes at Ian while Jess and Colin looked back and forth between them, their jaws hanging open. Colin dropped his arms and then wordlessly gestured between the two.

"Dude!" Cass said.

"It's not like they'll ever believe us anyway, Cassidy," Ian said, rolling his eyes.

"No, that makes perfect sense," Colin said, holding up a finger. Finally he stepped farther into the room and flopped on the couch. "Because Ian sat on the bench all throughout soccer practice and Cass didn't do her vocal warm-ups this morning."

Cass and Ian turned on each other, their mouths hanging open, their eyelids little slits.

"You said you'd do my warm-ups," Cass whined, as much as Ian's voice could whine.

"Well, I am not a benchwarmer, Cass," he complained back at her. "You were supposed to play for me."

She put her hands up in the air. "Like I was going to play soccer. Did you want all your friends laughing at you?"

"I can't believe this!" Ian shouted.

"Wait a minute," Jess said slowly. She pointed at Ian and said, "I can't believe you let me take you bra shopping."

Colin and Cass both gasped at the same time. Colin jumped off the couch and grabbed Ian's arm. "Did you see my girlfriend naked?"

Ian's face flooded with heat and he swallowed hard. "Not by choice." He turned to Jess. "I tried to get out of it. You *know* I did. I don't understand why girls have to go in the same change room together. It doesn't make any sense."

With wide eyes, Jess put her red face in her hands. "You should have said something…"

"Wait, wait," Cass said, holding up her hands to get everyone to calm down. "Do you guys actually…believe us?"

Colin and Jess exchanged a quick, odd glance with each other. Jess said, "Yes, we do."

"And I'll tell you right now," Colin said, "you guys have to be nice to each other."

"What is that supposed to mean?" Cass sputtered. "I'm always nice to him. *He's* the idiot."

Colin lifted an eyebrow while Jess giggled.

"Yeah, sure, Cass," Jess said. "Look, if you guys want to switch back, you're going to have to…be nice and, I don't know…"

"Learn each other's thing?" Colin filled in.

She smiled up at him. "Yeah. Learn each other's thing."

For a moment the air around them stilled as they continued to gaze lovingly into each other's eyes. Finally, Cass cleared her throat, the sound thundering around the room and snapping Colin and Jess out of their trance.

"Could you guys like not be disgustingly cute right now?" she said, glaring at them. "Ian and I need serious help here."

"Sorry," Jess murmured. She came closer and took Cass's hands, weird as it felt in that moment. "You're really going to have to figure this out on your own, though, Cass. I don't think it'll work if we help you."

"What are you talking about?" Cass asked. She was relieved that Jess and Colin believed them, but it still didn't seem to be all that helpful.

"It's like, some sort of magic," Jess said.

"It's meant to make you resolve your differences," Colin said. "I think, anyway."

"How could you possibly know that?" Ian asked.

Jess dropped Cass's hands and turned to Colin who shrugged. She said, "This...happened to us. Me and Colin."

Cass looked over at Ian, who wore a matching incredulous look on his face. "That can't be..." Cass trailed off.

"It can't?" Jess asked, raising an eyebrow.

Cass looked back and forth between her best friend and her brother. "When? How come I didn't know?"

"It was the summer before Ian and I started grade ten," Colin explained. He sat back down on the couch and rubbed a hand over his hair. "We had that big soccer tryout..."

"And I had that dance recital," Jess added.

Cass slumped onto the couch next to Colin and said quietly, "And we had our first date..."

"You guys were so weird that week," Ian said as he sat on the other side of Colin.

Jess giggled and took the last spot on the couch beside Cass. "From the outside, yes, we acted very oddly."

"The only way we got through it was to just be each other," Colin said. "I learned to dance and she got first string for me."

"Ian," Cass said suddenly. "Your soccer game..."

He sighed. "It's the same day as your audition, isn't it?"

"Yes," she said.

"Well..." Colin said.

"Yeah, huge problem there, buddy," Ian said. "I can't sing."

"Well, *you* can't," Cass said. "But *I* can."

Ian leaned forward on the couch so he could look at the others and threw his hands up in the air. "Do you see? You see why this won't work? She hates *everything* about me! How could she possibly do anything to help me out?"

While Cass was flailing around for any words that would appropriately negate him, Colin said calmly, "I wouldn't say she hates everything about you. I did catch her checking herself out in the locker room earlier."

"*Colin!*" Cass smacked Colin's arm, the force of it greater than she'd anticipated. "I wasn't checking myself out. I was—" She cut herself off as heat flooded her face. She rubbed her five-o'clock shadow to try to get rid of the blush. "I was trying to get your cup just right so you wouldn't get hurt during soccer practice."

Jess made a little sound of assent. "See? She does care a little."

Though he wanted to admit that that was kind of nice of her, what Ian said instead was, "How hard could it be? It can't be nearly as complicated as putting on a bra."

"Uh..." Jess stood up and reached out for Colin's hands. "I think maybe now is a good time for us to leave you guys alone."

"Yeah..." Colin got up when Jess tugged on his hands. "I really don't want to hear more about cups and bras." He gave a little shudder.

"So, wait," Ian said before they left the room. "I'm guessing kissing didn't work for you guys either?"

Colin let out a little snort. "You guys kissed each other like that? Boy, we missed our chance, Jess."

Jess put her hands over her mouth but they could still hear the snicker that escaped. "Colin, we really should be serious about this."

Colin snorted again, putting his arm around her shoulders. He turned them around and started heading out of the room. "I can't help it. They kissed themselves!"

Jess let out a short bark of laughter, then looked over her shoulder at them, mirth still in her eyes. "Be nice to each other," she said, just before they disappeared through the doorway.

Cass and Ian, at opposite ends of the couch now, stared at each other, their faces matching shades of crimson. Eventually, when they realized that they weren't truly alone in their predicament, the colour faded away and so did their anger.

Ian finally broke the silence. "I'll teach you."

"Teach me what?" Cass asked.

"To play soccer. If you're willing." He looked down at *his* body. "We'll start with the cup and work our way down."

She let out a little chuckle and nodded. "Okay. I'll try my best."

Ian licked his lips and looked away. "And I'll—I'll try to do your audition. But I'm not sure I can land you a lead. I know nothing about music."

"That's okay." She scooted a little closer to him, her eyes shining. "Those songs are in there, deep inside my body somewhere. We'll just...start at middle C and work our way up."

"Up?" Ian asked.

"Yeah...'cause I'm a soprano?" Cass added. Ian just shook his head. "Oh boy, we've got a lot of work ahead of us."

CHAPTER SEVEN

Deciding that there was no time like the present, Ian and Cass sat at her piano. While she shuffled through her music, he nervously twisted up his hands. There was no way he would ever learn to sing like her—she had a powerful, beautiful voice that could make him cry if he let it. Whatever was he supposed to do with it?

"Okay, so I have two songs I'm auditioning with," she said, unaware of his internal struggle. "One is an upbeat pop song. The other is a slower show tune. To showcase that I can do both, you know?"

"Of course," he said. Didn't help him at all, but he at least understood what she meant. "Wishing You Were Somehow Here Again," he read off the first sheet.

She nodded. "Yeah, from *The Phantom of the Opera*. It's perfect for my—my voice. You'll catch on quick."

He scanned the first few lines quickly. "Cass, this song is super depressing."

"Mmmhmm—oh, hey look!" She stretched her hands out and hit a couple of notes on her piano. "You can reach over an octave. I'll never be able to do that."

"Right," he said, staring at the keys. "What's an octave?"

"Oh, boy." She spun around on the piano stool and put her head in her hands. "This is never going to work."

"What?" He shook her shoulder gently. "Come on, Cass. Let's just try this...super sad song, okay?"

"You don't even know what an octave is," she complained.

He rolled his eyes. "I don't need to to learn the song. I'm doing this for you, you know."

She pursed her lips. "Alright. Here, just sing along with the notes I play, okay?"

Ian did as he was told, trying to match the pitches she played while singing the correct syllables at the correct time. The song was vaguely familiar to him—he'd seen the musical before—but he'd never realized just how hard the song was.

But when it came to the chorus and Cass started playing some really high notes, he clamped his mouth shut. She lowered her eyebrows at him.

"Why'd you stop? You were doing alright," she said, albeit begrudgingly.

He shook his head, his eyes wide. "I can't sing those notes. There's no way."

"Yes, you can," she said on a sigh. "If I can, so can you. Try lifting your hand in the air."

Ian looked down at his hands twisting up together in his lap. "Are you serious right now?"

"I'm very serious," she said. He knew that tone of voice. "Reach your hands up when you go for those high notes. It helps you visualize."

He lifted one hand in the air but not terribly high. "Really?"

"Yes, really," she said. "Imagine it's like...following through on really hard kick. You wouldn't just hit the ball and then stop, right? No, you'd keep moving forward. It's like that."

He lifted an eyebrow at her. "So, you do know something about soccer."

She shrugged and placed her hands on the piano to start playing again. "I *have* spent years watching you and Colin play. And it's not like it's hard. I'll probably have a way easier time of it than you will learning my music."

"Uh, soccer is way more complicated than just singing, Cass," he told her.

She dropped her hands forcefully on the piano, the discordant sounds accompanying her fierce scowl. "*Just singing*? Okay, this is just not going to work. There's no way I'm doing your soccer thing if you're not going to take this seriously."

She got up from the piano and headed towards the front hall. He quickly followed, grabbing her elbow as she reached for the door.

"Wait," he said. "I'm sorry. Please. I never meant for it to sound like that."

She whirled around, an unmistakeable fire in her eyes. "You know, all I wanted after we broke up was some time and space away from you. But I hardly ever get that because you're always with Colin and always asking about me. And now *this*. This is the opposite of what I wanted. We're stuck in each other's bodies and I *still* can't get you to be serious about me."

There was a weighted silence as Ian considered her words. Had she always thought that about him, that he was never serious about her? Did she mean that he hadn't had serious feelings for her or that she felt he didn't take her seriously as a person? Either way, he thought she was wrong but he wasn't sure if it was worth it to point out.

When Ian took too long to answer, Cass whipped the door open and stomped over the threshold.

"Where are you going?" he asked. He figured he had a right to know, since she was taking his body out, after all.

"I'm going to learn to play soccer," she tossed over her shoulder, just before ducking into *his* car.

With a frustrated sigh, he went back inside and slammed the door shut. He flopped onto the couch that he'd sat in so many times before but now felt new and foreign in Cass's body. He closed his eyes, wondering what he was supposed to do with himself now.

He knew what he should do. He pulled Cass's phone out of his pocket and opened up her playlist. There at the top was "Wishing You Were Somehow Here Again." He put it on repeat, pressed play, and closed his eyes again.

* * *

Even though she'd said she was going to play soccer, instead Cass got into Ian's car and drove around aimlessly for a while. Eventually, she subconsciously took herself to Jess's house, the only other place that could provide her a modicum of comfort.

When she got there, she almost let herself right into the house. But then she realized that if anyone but Jess was home, then it would look awfully strange if Ian Stokes were to just barge in. So she rang the doorbell and waited, heaving a relieved sigh when Jess answered.

Jess's eyebrows rose up her forehead when she saw Cass before falling to their neutral position again. "What's up?" she asked softly.

Cass frowned, her lip quivering, and a tear fell down her cheek. "I don't want to be a boy."

"Awwww. Come here..." Jess put her arms around Cass, somewhat awkwardly, and squeezed.

She took Cass up to her room and shut the door. Taking her hands, she said, "It's kind of yucky in there, isn't it?"

Cass nodded mutely, sniffling as more tears fell. "Yeah...kind of..." She tried swiping at her eyes and nose to no avail until Jess offered her a tissue.

"Did you...think about what Colin and I told you guys?" Jess asked. "You know, about trying each other's things?"

"Yes," Cass said, blowing her nose one more time. "We sat down at the piano and everything. And all he did was complain and joke around. I can't work with him like that."

"I know," Jess said, patting her arm gently. "I know this is really hard. And don't hate me for saying this but...have you tried soccer yet?"

Cass shook her head. "But you know that's not nearly as hard or as important as my audition."

Jess's eyebrows shot up to her hairline. "How can you say that? You know it is to Ian."

Cass bit her lip and looked away. Of course she knew how important this game was to Ian, and to Colin, too. But Ian didn't seem to care just how very important her audition was to her. How was it fair that she had to take it seriously when he wouldn't?

"Look." Jess paused to squeeze Cass's arm. "The only person in the world who can sing your songs for you right now is Ian. And the only person in the world who can play that soccer game for him now...is you. You're gonna have to get over whatever happened between you in the past, and whatever's happening between you right now. It's the only way."

"I know you're right," Cass said quietly. "But how am I supposed to get him to be serious about it?"

Jess's eyes softened as she gave her a gentle smile. "I think you know the answer to that."

Cass nodded. She had to be serious about playing for him if she wanted him to do the same for her. "Okay..."

"Come on," Jess said, grabbing her phone. "We've watched them play lots of times. Heck, I've even played for Colin. We can figure this out. Let's see, you're a..."

"Centre forward," Cass said, completely resigned.

"Which means you...?"

"Better have good enough aim to score a bunch of goals at the game on Tuesday," Cass finished bitterly. Maybe this wouldn't be as easy as she'd told Ian it would be.

"Ah, see?" Jess grinned. "You've already got the basics. Now you just have to hack that rocking bod of yours to get it to do what it normally does."

"Ew, don't call it a rocking bod, Jess," Cass said, scowling down at Ian's body. Oh, how she wished she weren't stuck in it.

Jess smirked. "I think you've called it that once or twice before, haven't you?"

Heat flooded Cass's face, and she just *knew* how noticeable that would be on Ian's pale skin. "You just had to bring that up, didn't you?"

Jess's smile slipped and a little frown appeared between her eyebrows. "Can I tell you something, Cass? There are worse people you could have switched bodies with than Ian."

Cass crossed her arms over her chest and looked down at her feet. Maybe it wasn't the worst option. She did at least know Ian really well, so well she knew his schedule, his family, his eating habits, his style of playing soccer. And now she literally knew him inside and out. But still...

"But you *know* why we broke up," she reminded her friend. "I can't just so easily forget about that."

Jess chewed on her lip. "Not even to get back into your own body?"

Okay, that was a good point. "Maybe."

"Alright, so you're going to go home," Jess said. "Ian's home, that is. And watch every video you can find of how to play centre forward until you pass out. Okay?"

Cass nodded solemnly. She could do that.

"And then you have to actually *play* at his practice," Jess added.

"That part might be a bit harder..."

"Cass." Jess pushed her playfully. "If I can do it, so can you. Besides, Colin will be there, I'm sure he can help you out."

Cass gave her a weak smile and leaned her head on Jess's shoulder like she'd done so many times before. Only this time, her shoulder seemed farther away and smaller now. She sighed. "I wish I could sleep over."

"Well, that would be a disaster," Jess said wryly. She patted Cass's knee. "But I'm confident that if you just try—and set aside your differences—then you two can resolve this. Okay?"

"Alright." Cass stood up and headed for the door. She turned back and said, "Can you do me a favour and put some makeup on Ian tomorrow? One day is one thing, but two days in a row without?"

Jess smiled. "No problem."

"You're the best, Jess," Cass said. She shoved her hands in her pockets. "See you around?"

"Of course," Jess said.

CHAPTER EIGHT

Ian woke to classical music, determined to make today better than yesterday. And the only way he could think to do that was to follow Cass's routine as closely as he could. So, he got up and headed to her piano.

He would never be able to play the thing—at least not like her—and he couldn't read the notes on her music. But he could at least try to do her warm-ups and hope that there was some magic in the piano that would give him a boost.

He opened his mouth and start singing some oohs and aahs, but everything that came out felt weird and foreign to him. He tried again, in a higher pitch and louder tone. He stopped abruptly when he heard Colin's thundering footsteps coming towards him.

Ian spun around on the piano bench just as Colin slid into the room, his eyes wide and frantic.

"What are you doing?" Colin asked, his eyebrows squished together.

"Exercises?" Ian said timidly. He knew Colin had a tendency to make fun of Cass for them, but this seemed a little excessive.

"That's *not* what her exercises sound like," Colin said as he plopped down next to Ian. "You're gonna wreck her voice."

Ian swallowed down his guilt and embarrassment. "I didn't know you cared that much," he said to cover up his feelings.

Colin scowled. "She's my sister." He moved some sheets around on the music stand until he found the one he wanted. "Here, this is one she usually does."

Ian crossed his arms and glared at the page. Dots and lines on more lines with a bunch of arches. "You know I can't read that."

"Didn't Cass teach you anything yesterday?" Colin asked.

"Not really," Ian said, though it was a half truth. "She just got all huffy and left." Okay, that was even less truthful.

Colin sighed, his shoulders dropping. "I can't believe I'm doing this... Here, sing what I sing."

Colin opened his mouth and sang a sweeping up and down melody to a simple ooh while Ian stared at him. Colin interrupted himself midline to say, "*Sing.*"

That prompted Ian to try too, but he couldn't figure out how to hit the notes Colin was singing.

Colin rolled his eyes. "In your octave, not mine."

"*What* is an octave?" Ian asked, throwing his hands up into the air.

Colin narrowed his eyes but then a tiny smile grew on his face. He played two notes, one high and one low, on the piano and said, "This. This is an octave. I'm singing this note and you need to sing this one."

"Ohhh," Ian said, sort of finally putting it together. He waited for Colin to start singing again and sang with him. He could hear now that the notes were the same, only his voice was higher than Colin's.

"That's better," Colin said, visibly relaxing.

"I...didn't know you could sing," Ian said, seeing Colin with new eyes.

Colin raised an eyebrow, a smile playing at his lips. "I can't. This isn't singing. This is warming up. Even you could do it... I mean, in your own body, that is."

Ian shook his head. He wasn't so sure of that. "But you *can* sing."

Colin shrugged. "Not according to anyone that's heard Cass. Oh, speaking of Cass, she's probably waiting for me." He stood up and started for the doorway. Just before he left, he said, "Please don't wreck her voice. We'll never hear the end of it if you do."

Ian laughed. "I'll do my best."

Once Colin was gone, Ian tried the exercise a few more times. He got it now—it was completely different than what he'd been trying in the first place. After that, he tried the chorus of "Wishing You Were Somehow Here Again," the part that he'd told Cass he couldn't do yesterday. But as it turned out, he could actually do it. And it wasn't...horrible. Probably not as good as if she'd done it, though.

He went back up to Cass's room to get ready and once again found himself facing a myriad of products he would never understand. He closed his eyes, trying to picture what her face normally looked like. But when he opened his eyes and looked into the mirror, what he saw was...perfect.

"Knock knock."

Ian whirled around so quickly he almost tripped over a pile of Cass's clothes on the floor. "Jess! What are you doing here?"

She smiled at him and then frowned as she carefully picked her way through the mess that was Cass's room. "I promised Cass I'd do your makeup before school."

Ian looked back at the mirror. "She doesn't need all that junk."

"Maybe not," Jess said as she started looking through the little bottles on Cass's vanity table. "But it isn't really for you to decide. You said you'd be her while you figure this out, right?"

"Yes..." He hesitated. "But look at her. She's beautiful."

Jess's face brightened up. "Now *that* we can both agree on. Don't worry, I'll go light on it, okay?"

"Fine," he said, resigned.

He sat down at the vanity table and tilted his face up towards Jess. She dabbed a bit of something on his cheeks and forehead, swiped a brush across his nose, then jabbed a stick into his eyelids.

"Ow."

"Sorry."

"I thought you said you'd go light," he complained.

"This *is* light," Jess said as she carefully applied some mascara.

"Just don't cover all her freckles, okay?" he said, regretting the words almost immediately.

Jess stopped fiddling with her tools and said, "Why don't you just tell her you're still in love with her?"

He wanted to lie and say he wasn't, but Jess would know better. She obviously already did. He sighed. "Like she'd listen to that."

"Maybe she would," Jess mumbled softly.

"Thanks for your help," Ian said, pushing Jess's hand away.

"I wish I could help you more, but…"

"Yeah, yeah," he said. "We have to figure it out on our own."

"Cheer up," she said, putting Cass's makeup away. "It's Friday. And the girls are going out for milkshakes after school. I know you never drink them around Colin, so…"

Ian smiled, his first real smile in the last couple of days. "You really know how to cheer a girl up, Jess."

She giggled. "Come on, let's get to school."

* * *

When Colin and Cass entered the school, they were greeted by Colin and Ian's friends in a typical boy fashion. Some of them rubbed Cass's head so hard it make her brain feel like it was knocking around in her skull. But once Cass realized they were being genuinely friendly, she laughed and pushed back a little. But not too hard, because Ian was a lot stronger than he looked.

"Oh, there's Christy," Colin blurted out. "Don't look at her."

"What?" Cass asked, looking directly at Christy surrounded by her group of friends. "Why not?"

"Just don't," Colin said. Using his entire body, he steered Cass away from Christy and down a different hall.

"Why?" Cass asked, smirking. "Are you worried if I give her the smoulder she'll fall in love with Ian or something?"

Colin lowered his eyebrows at her, scolding her with a single look. "Quite the opposite," he said in a low voice. "Ian's been trying to work up the nerve to ask her out for weeks. Don't screw it up for him, okay?"

Cass's heart plummeted to her stomach as she stared at her brother. So Ian really was planning on asking Christy out. He really was...over her, despite what Colin thought. "Oh...okay. Right. I don't want to mess that up for him."

Colin gave her a sympathetic smile and put his hand on her shoulder. "Sorry, sis." Someone walked by them then, so Colin punched her shoulder and said, "See you at practice, man."

Cass nodded and walked away dejectedly. Great. As if being in Ian's body couldn't get any worse. Now she was in his body and another girl was lusting after her ex-boyfriend. Well, no matter. She held her head high, determined to not think about it. She just had to get through this until they...

What if they never switched back? There was no way she'd go out with Christy if she was stuck like this forever. And she wouldn't want to play soccer for the rest of her life. She put a hand up to her throat. It wasn't as if she could live as a singer anymore either.

Don't cry, Cass, she told herself as tears burned behind her eyelids. *You have advanced calculus to worry about.*

Cass had a slightly easier time getting through Ian's classes. All she had to do was force herself to relax, sit at the back, and stay quiet for the most part. The teachers hardly ever called on her and, even though some of Ian's friends liked to goof off, they didn't care if she didn't.

She did hit a snag in his ancient history class when the teacher started off by handing them a quiz. She had no idea what most of the answers were. If Ian had told her ahead of time, she could have actually studied.

Cass shook her head at the thought. She was *not* going to be stuck here forever. There was no way she could take his final exams in a month. Oh! And he couldn't take hers either! Maybe the math and English ones he could pass since he'd been there before. But her vocal exam?

She bolted up from her seat and handed in her terribly completed quiz. She quickly left the classroom and headed straight for the boys' locker room. She had to play soccer. It was the only thing she could think to do if she wanted to get back into her body. She hoped Colin and Jess were right, that they really would switch if they did each others' things.

With a start, she wondered if Ian was doing that for her. But she couldn't think about that right now. There was still the issue of the cup to deal with before she got out onto the field.

The other guys started filtering into the locker room just as Cass was pulling her shorts on. As soon as Colin came in, his eyes found hers as if he just knew she'd be there waiting for him.

"Can we talk?" she said quietly to him as the others started getting ready.

"Yeah, what is it?" he asked.

He started undressing so Cass looked away. "I can't get it on right," she said under her breath.

Colin looked her up and down before he glanced around the room. Some of the others had already started leaving. He held up a hand and whispered, "Okay, in a minute."

They lingered, pretending to still be getting ready, until everyone had gone. When they were alone, he said, "Alright, show me."

She stood unmoving. "This is awkward."

He shrugged but she could tell it was a forced movement. "It wouldn't be the first time Ian showed me his junk..." he muttered.

She scrunched up her face and asked, "But why?"

"Cass." He put his hands on his hips and looked straight at her crotch. "Can we hurry this along? Coach'll bench us if we're late."

"Sorry," he mumbled. She pulled her shorts halfway down, her face heating up by a million degrees. At least this was just her brother and not some random person.

He took one look and said, "It's upside down, you dork. See you out there."

After he left her there, she quickly fixed the cup and then rushed to get outside. Colin was right—she couldn't be late. It would reflect poorly on Ian, and as much as she hated being inside his body, she didn't want to ruin his life.

"Stokes!" Coach called, looking exasperated. "There you are. Get on the field!"

Centre forward. She could do this. She'd spent all that time watching videos last night, had spent years watching Colin and Ian play. This should be easy.

She took her position and waited. As soon as the coach blew his whistle, she headed for the ball. Her brand new cleat caught on an uneven patch of grass and she fell face-first into the field. A strong hand gripped her upper arm and pulled upwards. When she stood up, she was face-to-face with Colin.

"Get your head in the game," he hissed before jogging away.

Head in the game. Right.

She got back into position and, paying close attention to what her feet were doing, started for the ball again at the whistle. She didn't get it, but she tracked it with her eyes. When it made its way to Colin, he immediately kicked it to her. It was like he knew exactly where she was.

With a little thrill of joy, she managed to catch the ball with her foot and started taking it towards the goal. With a great amount of oomph, she kicked as hard as she could...and watched it go wide of the goal post by at least two feet.

She let out a frustrated sigh, but the play continued and she had to stay focused. This would take a lot of getting used to.

CHAPTER NINE

Ian didn't have too much trouble getting through his classes for the day. He'd already been here and done most of this. And what he didn't know he could fake. Yet, being stuck as Cass made him feel mentally exhausted as he tried to navigate through her female friendships. He didn't want to act weird but he also didn't know whether joining in would make them think differently of Cass.

When they all went out for milkshakes after school—the one bright spot in his day—he was blindsided by a full-blown investigation into whether the new guy was hot or not.

"His nose is kind of off-centre," Ashley said, scrunching up her own little nose.

"But that just makes him cuter," Gina said. She turned to Ian and said, "Cass thinks Dylan's cute, right?"

When Ian shrugged, Jess elbowed him hard and said, "No, Cass thinks he's hot. There's a difference."

Ian choked on a snarky reply and quickly started downing his milkshake before he said something stupid. "Um, I need the bathroom," he said.

He rose so suddenly, he almost knocked over the table before rushing away towards the washroom. He checked to make sure he was alone and then, leaning over a sink, stared at himself in the mirror. Or rather, he stared at Cass's beautiful face, his heart torn in two. How could she be falling for someone else when he was still so in love with her?

The washroom door opened, so he turned on the tap to pretend he was washing his hands. But when Jess came to stand next to him, he turned the tap back off and sighed. She patted his back a couple of times and waited for him to speak.

"Does she really think he's hot?" He tried to speak quietly, but the question still bounced around the ceramic tiles of the washroom walls.

"Yes," Jess answered. Ian lowered his eyebrows at her and she laughed. "Come on. You guys have been broken up for months. She's not allowed to look at other boys?"

"No," he said forcefully. But he knew what a ridiculous sentiment that was, how stupid it sounded as soon as he had said it. "I mean...maybe. But..."

"But what?" she asked. "You're the only one who's allowed to look at other people?"

He scowled at her reflection. "What are you talking about?"

"Christy?"

"Ugh. You and Colin need to not talk to each other sometimes, you know?" he said to her.

She laughed. "We talk about everything. Sorry. Come out soon, okay? Otherwise everyone's going to think something's wrong with Cass."

Ian nodded and then followed Jess out of the bathroom. When they got back to their table, the girls had thankfully moved on from the topic of cute boys.

"Are you ready for your audition, Cass?" Gina asked, flipping her dark hair over her shoulder.

Ian shrugged. "Almost."

"Almost?" Gina laughed. "Please, they're probably going to beg you to do every part after they hear you sing."

"Then you can do a one-woman show!" Ashley said, laughing, too.

Ian smiled. "You think?"

"Obviously," Gina said. "You're the most talented person alive. Anyway, I gotta go, ladies. Too much homework."

"Same," Jess said, picking up her backpack.

"And I think I need to go practice some more," Ian said, truthfully meaning it.

* * *

As Cass and Colin got changed with the other boys from the soccer team, Cass once again kept her head down. Other girls might have liked the view, but to be honest, they were all sweaty and grass-stained and it wasn't a good look for any of them.

"You want to come over?" Colin asked her.

It was a simple enough request, phrased in a way that wouldn't sound weird to any of their teammates. But it made Cass want to cry. Of course she wanted to go home; that was where she felt most comfortable. But now she needed an invitation to do that and it was just so unfair.

She nodded, chewing on her lip to keep the sob in.

After a shower—as quick as she could manage—she gathered Ian's things and waited for Colin. Some of the other guys left her with parting gifts similar to their greetings: roughly rubbing her head, pushing her until she almost fell over, and affectionately calling her gross names that she would never use on her female friends. All with big smiles on their faces. It was kind of...sweet.

Cass led Colin out to Ian's car, where Colin hesitated. "I really wish you'd let me drive," he said, his hand on the passenger side door handle.

Cass smirked at him. "Why? You said it yourself, I'm a better driver than Ian is."

"I said that I thought *Ian* was driving better," he said. He huffed as he watched her get into the driver's seat and had no choice but to follow her. "If I'd known it was you, I might have never gotten in the car."

Cass pulled on her seatbelt and started the car up. "Why are you so much nicer to Ian than you are to me?"

"I'm not," he said. "I helped you out today, didn't I?"

"Yeah, but not for my sake," she said. "That was so that I could play like Ian, so Ian wouldn't look weird, so Ian will play well during the game. Not for me."

"Okay, well, I showed him how to do your vocal warm-ups this morning," he said as he reached for the radio. Noisy music blared from the speakers. "So that he wouldn't wreck *your* voice. Can we please go home, now?"

Cass put the car into gear, thinking about what Colin had said. Had he really shown Ian her warm-ups? "That was nice of you, thank you."

"Well, also he sounded awful," he said.

"What, like a dying ostrich?" she asked as she pulled out of the parking lot. That was what Colin usually said about her.

"I wish," he said. "No, that's you. He just sounds like death. Or at least he did, until I fixed it. You're welcome."

"Gee, thanks, Colin," she muttered, braking a little too hard at a stop sign.

He gripped the handlebar dramatically and shouted, "Watch what you're doing, Cass!"

"Oh, you'll live," she said, waving a hand in the air.

He grabbed her hand and put it back on the wheel. "Just drive," he grit through his teeth.

She stopped talking to focus on her driving and they made it home without incident. "See?" she said with a smug smile. "We're totally fine."

He snorted. "Fine is one way to put it." He stepped through the front door of the house and stopped suddenly, making Cass bump into him.

"What—?" She cut her own question off as a sound, beautiful and light made its way up from the basement to them. Her jaw dropped to the floor as she heard her own voice reach for the highest notes in "Wishing You Were Somehow Here Again." She couldn't believe it. Ian was actually...good.

Colin elbowed her. "You hear that, right?"

She blinked a few times to clear her eyes. "Yeah, he's...he's actually doing it."

He smiled. "I'd say he's more than just doing it."

"Colin?" a voice called from the kitchen.

Cass and Colin looked at each other and whispered together, "Mom."

They made their way into the kitchen where their mom smiled warmly at both of them. Cass wondered what it meant that her mom was still so nice to Ian. Granted, Ian had been Colin's best friend forever. But things were still a little different now that he and Cass had dated and broken up...right?

"Hi, Ian. How are you?" she asked kindly.

Cass smiled. At least she could always say her mom was the friendliest mom. "I'm fine, Mo-Mrs. Jacobs. How are you?"

"I'm great," she said. "Just about to head out to another showing, but I have time to make a snack if you boys are hungry."

"Yes," Cass said while Colin said, "No."

Mrs. Jacobs chuckled and went over to the fridge. "Ian says he's hungry, so I'll get you both something." She winked at them before getting out some things to make sandwiches.

"Thanks, Mom," Colin said as he sat at the table.

Cass sat across from him and continued listening to Ian sing. He hit a flat note but then to her surprise, he backtracked and tried it again. Ah, yes—the second time was much better.

"Here you go," Mrs. Jacobs said, handing them each a plate. "Listen...Cass is really in the zone right now and I haven't heard her practice like this in a few days. So don't bug her, okay?" She gave Cass a side glance and it warmed Cass's heart to know her mom was looking out for her.

"We won't," Cass said a little too quickly.

"But please do make sure she eats something when she's done," Mrs. Jacobs continued. "You know how she gets." She kissed Colin on the top of his head and started heading out of the kitchen.

"Will do," Colin said. "Love you, Mom."

Cass shoved her sandwich in her mouth before she blurted out the same thing. She definitely did love her mom, but it would be weird for Ian to say that. They ate quietly while Mrs. Jacobs got ready to leave.

Once she was out of the house, Colin turned to Cass and said, "Okay, go down there and get Ian to teach you how to score a goal."

Cass hesitated. Ian was just going over the ending of the song and he sounded so good. Better than she imagined he would. "But...Mom was right, he's in the zone. I can't interrupt him like this."

"The song's almost done," he said dismissively. "And his aim is way better than yours, so..."

"Okay, you're right." She nodded. "I'll go."

"And I better not hear any arguing," he said.

She smirked at him. "So put your earplugs in."

She crept slowly down the stairs so that she wouldn't startle Ian while he finished off the song. The last note was a bit strained and he needed to hold it a little longer, but other than that, it was a beautiful finish.

"Ian," she said softly.

He nearly fell off the bench with how quickly he tried to turn around on it. His eyes wide, he tried to say nonchalantly, "Oh, hey, Cass."

"Ian...that was beautiful," she said.

He lifted an eyebrow. "What, the way I almost fell?"

She chuckled and came closer to sit next to him. "No, the song, silly. It was great. When...when did you learn it? Like, *all* of it?"

He shrugged. "I listened to it on repeat for hours last night. It'll be forever stuck in my head now."

"Wow," she said, laughing a little more. "That's amazing. I mean...way better than—"

"Than you thought," he said quickly. "I know."

"No." She reached out and took his hand. "Way better than I did, is what I was going to say. No amount of watching soccer videos made me any good at scoring goals."

"Oh," he said, his whole face falling.

"I'm sorry," she said quickly. "I really tried so hard. You can even ask Colin. But I have terrible aim, apparently."

He smiled at her and ran his thumb along the inside of her wrist. "I think we can work on that."

She looked at their hands. She liked the feeling...a *lot*. Feeling horribly awkward, she jolted up from the bench and turned away from him. "Great. No time like the present, eh? Let's go out and kick some soccer balls."

He laughed. "Okay. Whatever you say, *Ian*."

They went back upstairs and Ian led them to the front hall closet. "There's gotta be a ball in here somewhere, right?"

"Top shelf," Cass said. Then she snickered while she watched Ian try to reach one of the balls that was just out of his reach. *She* had no problem getting it down, however. "Here you go, little lady."

"Very funny," he muttered as he took the ball from her. "Colin?" he called out.

"In the kitchen," Colin called back.

"We need a goalie," Ian said as they passed by the kitchen table towards the back door.

Colin was bent over a textbook and he looked up at them with a scowl. "I'm not a goalie."

"You are today, big bro," Ian said with a smirk. When Colin didn't move an inch, he said, "Please, man? For me?"

"And me?" Cass added.

"Ohhh…" Colin groused. "Fine. But if you don't get a goal in ten minutes, I'm coming back to my homework. I want to graduate, you know?"

Ian smiled and slapped him on the back. "We all do."

CHAPTER TEN

Colin gave her ten minutes to score a goal, but after twenty it was clear that this was a lot harder for her than they had realized. Ian couldn't figure out why, though, and it became increasingly frustrating watching a boy that looked just like him play so horribly.

"Cass." He sighed for the fifteenth time. "The goal is...*huge*. What's going on?"

"I don't know, Ian," she snapped. "I've never done this before."

"You've been doing it for the last half hour," Colin griped from where he was lying down between their makeshift goalposts. They had put two sticks in the ground roughly marking the distance between real goalposts. Cass had knocked each one over at least once, but still had yet to get the ball between them.

With an annoyed grunt, Cass kicked the ball, her eyes trained on her brother's face. The ball flew through the air, landing squarely on his stomach and then bouncing off him.

"Oof!" Colin jumped to his feet. "Cass!"

"I'm sorry," she said, her eyes wide.

"Don't be sorry," Ian said, rushing over to her with a huge smile. "You did it! You got it in!"

He put his arms around her and she couldn't help returning the hug. "I really did, didn't I?"

"Yeah," he said. Her arms were still around him as he smiled up at her. He pulled away a little too roughly. "Now let's do that like 50 more times. What'd you do differently?"

She shrugged. "I don't know. I was just looking at Colin and then I kicked the ball and—"

"Wait a minute," Colin piped up. He came over to them with the ball. "Are you saying you *haven't* been looking at the goal the whole time we've been practicing?"

"No..." she answered.

Ian scrunched up his whole face. "Then what have you been looking at?"

"The ball?" she said timidly.

They both stared at her and then Colin started laughing. He slapped Ian on the back—a little too hard considering how he almost fell over—and said, "That's on you, man. That's like, the first thing you were supposed to tell her."

"I figured she knew that already," Ian said, putting his hands on his hips.

"I'm right here," Cass said. "And I was watching the ball so I would kick it right. I didn't know there was any other way."

Colin laughed some more and shook her shoulder. "Watch where you want the ball to go. I'm going to finish my homework now. You kids be good. No more kissing."

Cass scowled and rolled her eyes as he walked away. But when she looked back at Ian, he was watching her with a strange expression on his face. "What?" she asked.

"Nothing," he said on a sigh. "Colin was just teasing, give him a break. Come on, try again. And look where you want the ball to go, not where it is."

"How am I supposed to know where it is if I don't watch it?" she asked. This was becoming exhausting, even in a well-toned body.

"Well, when you're on the field, of course you have to watch the ball," he said, trying to keep his voice gentle. "But when you're passing or trying to score, you really need to watch your target. Does that make sense?"

"I guess," she said. But she didn't move to kick the ball again.

"Come on," Ian said softly. "If my dumb brain can figure out where all the ridiculous notes in your song go, then I'm sure you can figure this out."

Cass sighed and picked up the ball to reposition it. "You're not dumb and those notes aren't ridiculous. They make perfect sense in the context of the whole song."

"And this makes sense in the context of the game," Ian said. "Go ahead. Score your goal."

Cass swallowed hard. If she couldn't get this, the very thing that Ian was trained to do and did well, then she might as well give up. She gathered her courage, kept her eye on the centre of the goal, and kicked as hard as she could. The ball flew in a perfect arch straight through the goalposts, landing well on the other side and rolling away.

"Cass, that was perfect!" Ian shouted as he once again put his arms around her in a tight hug.

She laughed and hugged him back. "Really?"

"Yeah, that was exactly how I would have done it," he told her. "It's a little harder with a goalie there, but we'll worry about that tomorrow."

"Tomorrow?" she asked.

"Yeah." He jogged over to the ball. "We always have Saturday practice before the big game. It's at ten. Sorry."

"That's okay," she said.

He kicked the ball to her and she stopped it with her foot without even thinking.

"Hey, that was pretty good," he said.

She grinned. "Thanks!"

Ian watched Cass make a few more goals before asking, "So, what am I doing tomorrow?"

She hesitated. "Well...I was going to go shopping with Jess, but she may not want to do that with you now. Other than that, I literally have to rehearse all day. You still have another song to learn."

"What's the other song?" Ian asked.

Cass smiled. "It's called 'Fidelity' by Regina Spektor."

"Of course," Ian said with a little laugh. "She's only your favourite singer ever. I guess I'll listen to that a million times tonight."

She clasped her hands together. "Really, Ian?"

He shrugged. "I have no other way of learning it."

She frowned and kicked the ball again, expertly knocking it through the centre of the goal. "But I mean...you're really that willing to learn my songs?"

He turned to her sharply. "Cass, don't you know...don't you know that I would do anything for you?"

Her frown deepened and she had to look away as tears rose unbidden to her eyes. Not this again. She couldn't handle Ian being all sweet when he... No. she wouldn't go there again. Not with him.

"I think maybe I need to go and practice by myself now," she said quickly turning towards the house.

"Wait," he said, reaching out to grasp her arm. "Don't you at least want to help me practice your songs?"

With more force than she meant, she pulled her arm away from him. Keeping her gaze on the ground, she said, "You're doing just fine on your own."

"I'm *not* fine on my own," he snipped.

Finally, she looked back at him only to find her own eyes filled with fire and...disappointment. She knew they weren't talking about practicing anymore and she just couldn't have this conversation right now.

"Yes, you are," she finally said quietly. "Tell Colin I said goodbye."

And with that, she ran back to the house, wrenching the door open. She ripped through the house, ignoring Colin when he called for her. Though she could barely see through the tears that finally fell, she got into Ian's car and pulled it out onto the street. Only then did she wipe the tears away so she could see clearly enough to get back to his house.

Ian followed closely behind and made it to the front door just in time to see her rip away in his baby. But it wasn't the car he was worried about. It was her. What had he done so wrong that every time they got close again, she ran away?

"What'd you do to her?" Colin asked, his eyebrows lowered.

Ian turned to him, crossing his arms and matching his expression. "I still have *no* idea. Ugh."

He took out Cass's phone as he made his way up to her room. He chose Jess's number, shut the door, and waited for her to answer.

"Hello, *Cass*," she said in a pleasant tone. "What's up?"

"Girl talk," he said in his girliest voice as he flopped onto the bed. "I wanna know what happened between me and Cass."

There was silence on the other end of the line for so long Ian thought that maybe Jess was gone or hadn't heard him. Then she breathed out deeply.

"Haven't you and Cass already talked about that?" Jess asked slowly.

"Sort of," he said. "She mostly just called me a bunch of names and told me she couldn't trust me anymore and that was that."

"Are you sure?" Jess asked. "You weren't mean to her, too?"

"Maybe a little," he admitted. "While we were breaking up. But not before then and I want a proper explanation now."

She sighed again. "I can't, Ian. That's really something you need to work out with her."

"I've *tried*," he complained. Frustration rose up in his chest and spilled over into his words. "I've tried talking to her. I've tried being extra nice to her, I've tried giving her space. I've even asked Colin—he gave me the same answer as you did. And now I'm just tired of it. I'm tired of her acting so coldly towards me when I have no idea what I did to her."

"I'm sorry, Ian. That's rough."

"So you'll tell me?" he asked hopefully.

"Ummmm, no," she said gently. "No one will be able to explain it better than her. And also, I feel like it would be a total betrayal of her trust if I did that. Sorry."

Ian sighed and squeezed his eyes shut. "Then do you have any suggestions on how I can get her to tell me?"

"It's been a few months," Jess responded. "She might be more willing to open up if you ask her nicely and don't ruffle her feathers. And maybe especially now that you're, you know..."

"In her body?" he filled in.

"Yeah," she said brightly.

"Alright..." he said dubiously.

She chuckled. "Just try again and don't forget to be nice. Is there anything else you need? Help practicing your songs?"

"Jess." He sat up slowly on Cass's bed. "You're the best friend a girl could ask for."

LEARNING TO SING LIKE A GIRL

She laughed. "Thanks?"

"You're welcome," he said. "And thank you. I think I'm okay today, though. What are you doing tomorrow?"

"I usually like to watch Colin's Saturday practices," she said. "You could come..."

"I probably should anyway," he said. "See how Cass is doing. I'll meet you there, okay?"

"No problem! Goodnight, Ian."

"Goodnight, Jess." *Cass is lucky to have a friend like you.* He should have said those words, too, but he didn't.

Instead, he found 'Fidelity' in Cass's playlist and put it on repeat for the rest of the night. As the lyrics and beautiful melody played, he wondered—was the song about him? Had Cass ever really loved him? Or had she only ever found her place in music and lyrics? And did she ever wonder what it would have been like if they'd never had a relationship at all?

How was he ever going to get her to tell him what went wrong?

CHAPTER ELEVEN

As soon as the smell of lasagna hit Cass's nose, she sighed in relief. She could do dinner with Ian's family, no problem. Plus, Ian's body was constantly hungry. A nice full meal might actually settle some of the nerves she was feeling. And maybe it would distract her from her last conversation with Ian.

"You're late!" Mrs. Stokes called from the dining room.

Oops. "Sorry," she called back, making her way towards them. "I was practicing with Colin."

"How's Colin doing?" Mrs. Stokes asked as Cass seated herself.

"He's good," she answered. That much she could say without lying.

"And how's Cass?" Emma, Ian's little sister asked.

"Huh?" Cass answered, staring at Emma. Despite the five-year age gap between her and Ian, Cass could see the similarities between them. The light blue eyes, blond hair, and little smirk Emma was wearing were all very Ian-like.

"Didn't you see Cass while you were over at Colin's?" Emma asked. Her smirk faded into something more innocent the longer she watched

Cass.

"Uh, yeah, I did," Cass said. That wasn't technically a lie.

"Okay, time to say grace," Mr. Stokes said.

Cass bowed her head, grateful for the interruption. As Ian's dad prayed, she realized she should have been grateful for a lot more than that. It could have been worse—she could have swapped bodies with someone she didn't know, or someone horrible. Despite her protests, Ian wasn't the worst choice. But it was hard to feel to feel grateful for anything in her current predicament. Giving thanks for food to feed a body that wasn't hers didn't exactly appeal to her.

"So," Mr. Stokes said as soon as everyone had started eating, "are you and Col ready for the big game?"

Don't remind me, Cass thought to herself. "Of course," she said with Ian's trademark confidence.

Mr. Stokes chewed his food thoughtfully for a moment before saying, "Make sure you stay closer to the sidelines."

Cass stared down into her food, trying to figure out how that could ever be good advice. Ian was a centre forward, emphasis on *centre*. Finally, she decided to just ask, "Why?"

"So that the scouts can get a good look at you, of course," he answered, raising an eyebrow in her direction.

"Oh, and make sure you take some hairspray with you," Mrs. Stokes added, her eyes lighting up. "Maybe I'll just take it and do some touch-ups during the game."

"Touch-ups?" Cass asked, her brows knit together. She reached up to touch Ian's short, stylish hair. It had never looked anything less than perfect to her. Plus it was a soccer game, not a modeling competition.

"And for the love of all that's holy, clean your uniform and shoes first," Mr. Stokes said.

Mrs. Stokes tsked in agreement. "You should be doing that regularly anyway, but your father's right. It's important they be clean before the scouts see them."

Unable to tamp down her unruly temper, Cass blurted out, "You know they're there to watch me play and not look at my clothes and my hair, right?"

Both parents' eyes grew huge. Mr. Stokes shook his head, letting out a long breath. "You need to look good, too."

"I *do* look good," she retorted on Ian's behalf. "When I'm playing the game. That's what the scouts care about."

Mrs. Stokes harrumphed indignantly. "Well, make sure you don't let them see that attitude while you play."

Cass's jaw dropped. She couldn't believe this. Ian may not have been the best boyfriend, but he was a fantastic soccer player. Even she recognized that. It shouldn't have mattered what his hair and shoes looked like while he played and she couldn't believe his parents would say this kind of stuff to him. Were they always like that?

"Can I get a cat?" Emma asked out of the blue while Cass was still trying to think up a response.

"We've talked about this, sweetheart," Mrs. Stokes said, laying her fork down delicately across her plate. "You're not responsible enough for a cat."

"But I *can* be," Emma replied in the whiniest tone Cass had ever heard her use. "You just need to give me a chance."

"The litter would get all over the place," Mrs. Stokes replied, splaying her hands out in the air.

"I'll sweep it twice a day," Emma said earnestly.

"And who will pay for its food?" Mr. Stokes asked, glancing at Emma over his glasses.

Emma stabbed the last potato on her plate, her shoulders dropping dejectedly. "Fine. I'll wait until I get a job, then I'll get a cat."

She looked at Cass and winked. Cass couldn't help a tiny smile. Emma was looking out for Ian and she thought that was really sweet.

After dinner, while Emma was filling the dishwasher, Cass went to help her, but Emma elbowed her out of the way.

"You're in the way, Ian," Emma complained.

"I was trying to help," Cass said, her eyebrows drawn in in confusion.

"Well, it's my night," Emma answered, meticulously placing another plate into the dishwasher.

Cass stood there awkwardly, trying to decide what Ian would do in this situation. But right now, that didn't matter, because *she* was Ian. She was the one who had talked back to his parents so she was the one who Emma had rescued earlier.

"Thank you," she said softly.

Emma looked up at her, her eyebrows all scrunched together. "For what?"

Cass shrugged. "For saving me from, um, Mom and Dad earlier."

Emma rolled her eyes and leaned over to close up the dishwasher. "I can't believe you talked back to them like that."

Cass's face warmed up, turning a bright red. "I guess I shouldn't have."

Emma shook her head, a little smile playing on her lips. "No, you definitely should. And you know what else you should do? Decide what you're going to do with that half-painting."

Now Cass was totally lost in the conversation. "What are you talking about?"

Emma scoffed, flipping her hair over her shoulder. "Come on, Ian, don't be like this. I can reuse that canvas if we're not going to finish Cass's painting. Can we please decide now? It's been weeks."

Cass's heart picked up its rhythm. Was she supposed to believe that Ian and Emma were in the process of painting something for her? She knew Emma was artistic, but Ian had never been.

Choosing her words carefully, she said, "Let me take another look at it."

With one more sigh, Emma started in the direction of the garage. "Not sure how looking at it—*again*—will make any difference, but okay."

Emma led them to the garage, pulling back a curtain that sectioned off a corner of the room. Cass's eyes widened as she gazed upon what was evidently Emma's makeshift art studio. She'd had no idea Emma was that into painting. Cass tried to take it all in—the finished pieces that were amateurish but still nice depictions of wildlife. The brushes, palettes, and half-full paint tubes. The dirty smocks hang up on the wall.

Emma went over to an easel with a canvas that was covered by a sheet. She ripped the sheet off with a flourish and stood there with one hand on her hip. Cass gasped before she remembered to conceal her reaction.

She forced her facial muscles to relax even as she took in the sight before her. It wasn't finished yet, but she could tell it was the beginning of a painting of her and Ian in a familiar pose—the picture they'd taken in front of that silly statue.

She tried to even out her breathing. Ian must have been working on this before they broke up. But she guessed he couldn't give it up just yet because—because he still liked her?

What was she supposed to do now? She couldn't decide for Ian if he was ready to let this painting go, no matter what she felt about them or their relationship. And even if Emma was now tapping her foot impatiently, she just couldn't do that to Ian. It wouldn't be fair.

"Sorry, Emma," Cass said, turning to her. "I'm not ready yet."

"Yeah, figures," Emma said nonchalantly. "I'll ask again in a week."

Cass couldn't help laughing. "Thanks. What are you working on now?"

Emma hesitated, dropping her gaze to the ground. "If I show you, you'll make fun of me."

Cass took a little step closer and said, "I won't. I promise."

"Well..." Emma touched the cloth covering another canvas. "I was inspired..."

She pulled the cloth away, revealing a painting of a boy with brown skin and green eyes. He had a pleasant smile and a plaid shirt and Cass thought he looked terrific.

"Wow, he's cute," Cass blurted out without thinking.

Emma rolled her eyes. "I knew you'd make fun of me."

"I'm not, I promise," Cass said. She didn't care what Ian would say in this situation. Emma deserved to have someone tell her something nice about her artwork. "It's a really nice painting."

Emma looked at her for a moment before smiling. "Thank you."

"I won't ask who he is," Cass tried.

Emma smirked. "I wouldn't have told you anyway."

Cass laughed. She'd never really gotten a chance to get to know this side of Emma and she liked it. It wasn't exactly fun to be in Ian's body...but it was kind of fun having a little sister for a while. She hoped Ian would always treat her right.

Just before Cass went to bed, Colin texted her.

Colin: Run tomorrow morning?

Cass: Is that a thing I do on Saturdays now?

Colin: You bet!

With a groan, she rolled over and buried her face into Ian's pillow. This soccer thing *had* to work, otherwise she'd be stuck going for runs every morning with her brother for the rest of her life.

* * *

Saturday morning. Usually Ian would have gotten up early to go for a run with Colin. But after hearing him get up earlier, Ian took the opportunity to roll over and go right back to sleep. Cass had said she would normally have just been singing all day, but she didn't say when her day had to start.

Even after he heard Colin come home and go into the shower, he couldn't find the will to get up just yet. Instead, he found Cass's headphones and listened to 'Fidelity' again. He'd already memorized the music and lyrics last night. Today's listen was purely for the enjoyment factor. No matter what this song might mean to Cass, he still found that he liked it a lot.

Eventually, he did get up and go down to the piano. Not that he could play the thing—and he would probably never learn—but it felt more natural to practice here. He did the warm-ups that Colin had taught him until he felt like he could reach those high notes. And then he sang.

The whole time he practiced, he wondered if his singing would be good enough, if he could ever really pass for Cass like this. Was he doing it right? Hearing her voice from inside her head was totally different, a surreal experience that he wished he could do away with. But then, maybe that's how she felt playing soccer for him. Ugh, all this overthinking hurt his brain.

He went back up to finally feed himself. Mrs. Jacobs was in the kitchen, making some oatmeal, which she offered to Ian. He smiled gratefully and sat down with the bowl.

"I haven't heard you practice your piano in a few days," Mrs. Jacobs said as she sat across from him. "Don't you think you should focus on that before your audition, too?"

Ian shrugged. "I just want to make sure I get the singing right. That's what's most important, right?"

Mrs. Jacobs smiled, but it seemed a little forced. "Well, yes, but weren't you going to accompany yourself? We didn't get you an accompanist this time because you insisted you were confident enough to do it."

Ian dropped his spoon into his bowl with a clatter as he swallowed hard. *Why* hadn't Cass thought to mention that? What was he supposed to do now?

Mrs. Jacobs was giving him a strange look, so he giggled as he picked up his spoon. "Whoops. Yeah, I'll be totes fine, Mom. Don't worry about it."

But as much as *Cass* might have meant that, Ian's heart was pounding in his ribcage. Singing the songs for her was one thing—he could do that, especially if he were singing along with something. But there was no way he'd be able to learn those piano parts. He was great with his footwork, but knew he'd be totally uncoordinated on a piano.

He finished his breakfast quickly and then went upstairs to call Cass. But she wasn't picking up. He looked at the time—9:45. She was probably busy getting ready for soccer practice.

He called Jess instead, who answered with a perky "Good morning!"

"Hey, Jess," he said. "I'm coming to the practice with you."

"Sounds great!" she answered. "Meet you there?"

"I've already got my shoes on," he answered.

"Wait," Jess said. "Which shoes?"

"I don't know," he snipped. "The ones closest to the front door."

"Oh, okay. Those are fine," Jess said.

Ian rolled his eyes. "So glad to have your approval. See you soon."

"Bye," Jess said.

CHAPTER TWELVE

Once again, Cass was the last one out of the locker room. But this time it wasn't because she was trying to get everything adjusted right. No, it was because she was so nervous she was shaking. It was silly, really—the game wasn't even until Tuesday, which should have been plenty of time for her to...

Magically become the best player on the team. Yeah, that was something she could make happen between Saturday morning and Tuesday evening.

She blew out a long breath and rushed out onto the field with Ian's teammates. As soon as she got out there, Coach said to her, "Ian, take the bench."

Her eyes widened and Colin looked over sharply. "Wait, why?" she asked, trying not to sound belligerent.

Coach shook his head and couldn't quite meet her eyes. "I just don't know what's going on with you lately. Coming out late, missing passes and goals..." He shook his head again.

"No," Cass said, lifting her hands up in surrender. No, she couldn't let this happen to Ian. "I've just... I wasn't feeling well the last couple of days. But I'm one hundred percent today, I promise. Please give me one more chance." *And I better not blow it.*

Coach chewed thoughtfully on his lip.

"Come on," Cass said, lowering her voice. "You know I'm the best centre forward on the team."

Coach's eyes crinkled with a tiny smile. "Boy, if it were anybody else but you... Alright, Stokes, you get out there. But no more messing around. I want to see everything you've got for our game."

Cass grinned. "Yes, sir," she said a little too brightly.

Great. She had talked her way out of a problem just like Ian would have. Now she just had to play like him. She thought about how he had effortlessly belted his way through "Wishing You Were Somehow Here Again," hitting almost every note perfectly and going back for the ones he'd missed. If he could do that for her, then she knew she could coerce his body into playing soccer like it knew how to.

"Alright, guys, let's do this!" she called out to no one in particular, clapping her hands together.

Several of the guys called encouraging words back to her while Colin smiled and nodded. A funny thought occurred to her when she imagined Jess playing in Colin's position and she almost laughed out loud. That must have been terribly lonely for her and now she was glad that Ian had told Colin and Jess about their predicament.

Coach came to the centre of the field and flipped a coin, then gestured in Cass's direction. Her team would get the first play. Good. This was her chance to show them all how incredibly awesome...Ian was. How great a player her ex-boyfriend was.

No, there was no time to think like that. She just had to get through this practice as best she could and hope that was good enough for now. Of course, she had the advantage of playing with not only Ian's best friend but her very own brother.

After watching hours of soccer games, Cass knew now what imaginary spots on the field she needed to stick to. And when she was in the right position Colin always knew exactly where she would be when it came time to pass to her. Every single time, without fail, when he looked up so did she.

He would pass her the ball—which she was quite good at catching with her foot—and then she would nimbly move around the defense to get to the goal. She didn't make every shot she took, but she was proud to be able to score a fair number of them.

About halfway through the practice, Colin came close to her and said, "You're looking really good out there, but you need to loosen up a bit. You're too tense. Don't worry, you've got this."

Cass nodded, little droplets of sweat rolling down her face. "Thanks, Colin."

He slapped her on the back and they got back into position. It was only then that Cass noticed Jess and Ian on the bleachers watching them. Ian's mouth was slightly agape and he was staring at her with wide eyes. When he noticed her watching him, his whole face cracked into a grin. Cass couldn't help smiling back.

A whistle sounded and she refocused her attention to the game. She could do this. In fact, she *was* doing this. By the end of the practice, she was sweating and breathing heavily. But she knew she'd done far better than yesterday.

"Good hustle, Stokes," Coach said as he watched her come off the field. "That's more like it. Keep that up until Tuesday, eh?"

Cass grinned. "No problem, Coach."

She followed her teammates—no, *Ian's* teammates to the showers. She had played hard and she knew she needed to wash all of the sweat and grass off of her. As she attempted to shower, the other guys goofed off. And then of course, there was the towel-slapping. Cass groaned and side-stepped around the flailing towels.

Cass finished her shower as quickly as possible and looked around for Colin, who scowled at her and turned his back. She shrugged. It wasn't her fault he was taking too long getting dressed.

"See you guys later," she called out. The guys called back to her, complete with friendly insults.

She went back outside, followed by Colin, and found Jess and Ian waiting for them. Ian's whole face lit up when he saw her, so evidently they weren't fighting anymore.

"That was amazing," he said, clasping his hands together.

Cass smiled as heat warmed her chest. "Really?"

"You looked..." He paused and looked around them. The only people close enough to hear were Colin and Jess, and they were already starting to walk away hand-in-hand. "You looked just like me," he said quietly.

"Well," she said, smiling back at him, "after hearing you sing just like *me* yesterday, I guess I was inspired."

Ian's smile slowly disappeared. "Um, speaking of singing like you, your mom thinks you're accompanying yourself?"

"Oh." Cass's heart sank. Yes, now she remembered how much she had insisted that she could do it herself and didn't want to ask their 70-year-old neighbour to do it for her again. "Oh...shoot. Ian, I totally forgot about that. I was just going to go there and do it."

"I don't exactly have the time to learn piano," he said, his voice coming off a little testy.

"I know, I know," she said. She grabbed Ian's keys out of her back pocket and shook them. "Come on."

"Oh, my baby..." Ian muttered with a frown.

"You'll get over it," she said as they headed to the parking lot. "Now, shh, I'm trying to think."

"About what?" Ian asked.

"*The audition*," she said, giving him an exasperated look. "Unless you want to sing it a cappella..."

"Does that mean without music?" he asked timidly.

"Ugh, Ian." Cass rolled her eyes and shook her head. Looking down at her hands she said, "You know what? I'll just play with you."

"Um, don't you think people will find it really weird that a soccer player is so good at piano?" he said.

"Aw, you think I'm that good?" she asked.

Ian shook his head as they got closer to his parked car. "Focus, Cass. What if someone recognizes me?"

"At the theatre?" she asked, raising an eyebrow. "That's pretty unlikely."

He stopped and put his hand on her arm. "And your mom? Doesn't she usually go with you?"

Cass closed her eyes and groaned, the sound so low it almost startled her. "She *always* goes." Cass opened her eyes again and looked over to where Colin and Jess were leaning over Ian's car, kissing like they weren't in a parking lot. "Colin!" she called, snapping her fingers.

Colin nearly fell over with the barked command. He glared at her and said, "I can't figure this out for you guys. But you played very well today and I'm sure that'll help a lot."

Completely disregarding his comment, she said to him, "I need you to distract Mom during my audition on Tuesday."

"What?" he asked, his face all scrunched.

"I need you. To distract Mom. *During my audition*," Cass said, overexaggerating the words as she gestured heavily.

"Wow," Colin said, looking her up and down. "You know, your attitude in Ian's body is really unattractive."

Cass scoffed but before she could say anything, Ian said, "Colin, we're being serious. Do you want us to be stuck like this forever?"

Colin looked back and forth between both of them, a tiny smile growing on his lips. Jess elbowed him and he wiped the smile off his face. "What kind of distraction we talking about?"

"Anything that'll take her out of the building for a while so I can sneak in," Cass answered.

"Why do you need to sneak in?" Jess asked.

"I told my mom I'd accompany myself..." Cass admitted quietly.

Jess looked at Ian and said, "Ah...yeah, that would be a disaster."

"Oh!" Ian snapped his fingers. "Tell her you've got a calf cramp. That usually does it, right?"

Colin's eyes lit up. "Yeah, and I haven't used that in a while."

Cass and Jess exchanged the same I-can't-believe-what-I'm-hearing look with each other. "Wow, Colin," Cass said. "Were you lying all those times you told us that?"

He shrugged. "Not all of them. Look, do you want my help or not?"

"Yes," she said begrudgingly. "Alright...time for more practice." She unlocked the doors of Ian's car while the other three all looked at her. "Are you guys getting in or what?"

Ian sighed and reached for the passenger-side door at the same time as Colin. "Nice try," Ian said, jutting his thumb towards the backseat.

Colin slumped into the back with Jess and muttered, "Really wish you'd let me drive, Cass."

Cass smirked at him through the rearview mirror. "Nice try," she said, echoing Ian.

To her surprise, Ian actually laughed. "You're getting good at being me," he said.

She laughed, too. Was it a good thing? Maybe not, but...it also wasn't the worst thing.

CHAPTER THIRTEEN

Cass sat at the piano while Ian stood nearby. This surreal, out-of-body experience had only gotten weirder when he'd seen her playing soccer like an expert, like *he* would have. But now, as she put her hands to the piano and played a few notes, he breathed a sigh of relief.

This was the Cass he knew. The girl who felt completely at home on a piano bench, singing words that meant more to her than anyone would ever know. They weren't truly turning into each other, no matter how much they could act like each other.

She stopped playing to look over at him, still standing in the doorway. "Are you coming in or what?"

Ian nodded, chewing on his lip. She just had to snip at him, didn't she? "I was just watching you play, that's all. You don't need to be rude."

"I wasn't being rude," she said, narrowing her eyes. "I just didn't know why you were being all broody by the doorway."

"I wasn't brooding," he retorted, plunking down next to her on the bench. "Can we just sing the songs?"

She stared at him for a moment before saying, "We can't sing when we're all huffy at each other."

"Sure, we can," he said, scrunching up his face. "Watch." He opened his mouth and out came a note, scraggly and off-key. He clamped his mouth shut, his eyes wide. "Wow...you're right, it *is* hard to sing like that."

Cass laughed out loud. "Now you see why I hate being interrupted while practicing, why I don't like to be confronted when I'm training hard for something?"

Ian nodded. She was right—it was better for both of them to stay calm and not argue over things. "Yeah, I get it now."

She smiled at him. "Do you want me to teach you how to sing 'Fidelity' now?"

"I already know it," he said confidently.

"Oh, really?" she asked with an amused tilt to her head. "Let's hear it, then."

"Umm..." Ian cleared his throat and stared down at the black-and-white keys. "Can you play me, like—"

"An intro?" Cass asked, starting to play the opening chords.

"No," Ian said, placing one gentle hand on hers. "Just a first note would be okay."

"Okay," Cass agreed.

Though Ian couldn't tell the difference between one note on the piano and any other, Cass immediately played one. Then she looked at him with a little smile on her face.

So Ian sang a breakup song for his ex-girlfriend who was currently inhabiting his body. Cass kept her eyes on him the whole time, her smile growing bigger the longer he sang. He wondered if it had been this awkward, this vulnerable-feeling for Colin. What had he said? He'd had to learn to dance for Jess? Ian would have gladly chosen that over baring his—or Cass's—soul in song.

But after he'd finished and Cass clapped for him so delightedly, he could feel his face warm up from pride.

"Wow, that was so good," she said. "You even did it with that kind of airy quality Regina has when she sings it."

"That's...that's how you would have done it, right?" he asked uncertainly.

"Yeah, actually," she answered. "Do you want to try it with me now?"

Ian chewed on his lip. "Are you sure you're going to be able to sneak into the audition? What if Colin's calf cramp doesn't do it?"

"*Please*," she said, waving him off, "that's never not worked on Mom. Don't worry about it. Come on, I'm gonna do the intro."

Cass didn't wait. She turned back to the piano and started up the opening bars. But when Ian didn't come in when he was supposed to, she looped back to the beginning. Then she sang the first words.

Ian jumped right in—in the right octave this time—marveling at how Cass had managed to force his voice to sing anything passable. Cass's playing was easy enough to follow, but every once in a while he'd fumble over a pickup and she would sing for him.

"That was pretty good," Cass told him again. "The only part I really think you should work on is all those *betters*. I'd say it needs to be...better." She chuckled at herself but Ian just shook his head.

"There's just so many fast notes all in a row," he said, frowning. "Couldn't I cut some of them out?"

"No?" Cass answered, lifting an eyebrow at him. "It's not that bad. Listen."

She put her hands back on the piano, played the music, and sang the part in question. Her voice—or rather *his* voice—was a little rough, but she hit every note exactly where it belonged. His eyebrows hit his forehead as he listened to her.

"Wow," he said once she'd stopped singing. "I can't believe you did that with my voice! I didn't know..."

She smiled. "I mean...it's not...as horrible as I might have once thought. You have, you know, a regular baritone range, and with some amount of coaching you could probably sing something nice with it. I know that's not you, though."

"No," he said with laughter in his voice. "It's not me. It's you. I think you're literally the only person who could do that in my body. You're amazing, Cass."

She shrugged as pink crept onto her cheeks. "It's...it's the only thing I've ever known. You know that."

"Yeah," he said softly. "But you also just played soccer like it was the easiest thing in the world. So, it's not really me. It's you."

The red in her cheeks deepened and he giggled. That was why he'd always tried so hard to avoid embarrassing situations, but obviously compliments had the same effect on Cass. He put his hand up to her cheek, touching her gently.

"Ian." She grabbed his hand and put it back down in his lap. "Can you just try this part again and make it—"

"Better?" He grinned.

"Yeah," she said, laughing a bit.

She started at the beginning of the line to give him a good lead-in. This time, he sang every note, even all the tiny in-between ones that he'd never noticed in the song before he'd listened to it on repeat last night. And he had to admit—it sounded way better like that.

When Cass kept playing, he took the cue and finished the song with her. Afterwards she gave him another big smile.

"See?" she said. "You *can* sing."

"So I can," he said. She was still smiling at him. She was in a good mood. Maybe this was a good time to bring up...everything between them. "So...is this song about me?"

Cass just looked at him, the smiling slowly dissipating. Then she shook her head. "Yeah, Regina wrote this song after you broke her heart," she said dryly.

He swallowed back a nervous chuckle. "You know what I mean, Cass," he practically whispered.

Cass was silent for a minute as she touched the keys of her piano without actually pressing any of them down. Finally, she said, "I chose the song because it suits my voice well. Sure...I love the lyrics. I've always been most comfortable with my music and songs. That's what makes me happy. But does it remind me of you? No. At least it didn't. Now I'll probably never be able to think of it without thinking of you singing it for me."

Ian wiped his palms on his jeans. It wasn't quite the answer he was looking for, but it was better than nothing. "Okay," he said softly.

Cass swallowed hard, her Adam's apple bobbing up and down. "Let's practice some more, okay?"

"Sure," he said past the disappointment building in his chest. But he did his best to sing the song one more time for her. To make her happy. And to hopefully get himself back into his own body so he could finally leave her alone like she apparently wanted.

After another run-through of "Fidelity," they decided to try "Wishing You Were Somehow Here Again." This song was obviously the more challenging for Ian, but he could tell it was harder for Cass to play, too. It made him wonder why she'd chosen to accompany herself when she would have done a better job just focusing on her singing. But he didn't want to ask for fear that he'd get another disappointing and vague answer.

He sang the song along with her, watching her play the piano rather than reading the music since he'd already memorized the lyrics. Cass once again helped Ian to find the pickups, though she struggled a little more with this one. This song was definitely not in his voice's range.

After he'd sung the last note, she said, "That was really beautiful, Ian."

"Thanks," he muttered.

She eyed him and said, "This song's not about you either."

That got a laugh out of him. "I should hope not. I'm not dead yet."

"Not yet, no. Oh!" She turned to him suddenly, her knees knocking into his. "You *are* familiar with our regular lineup of church songs, right?"

Ian put his hands up to his face and groaned through his fingers. "Tell me I'm not singing in the church choir tomorrow."

"No, *you're* not," she said. "*I* am."

He sighed long and hard. "Cass...people might notice you messing up the songs."

"Don't worry," she said, putting her hand on his arm. "I'm a soprano, I just sing the melody. Should be pretty easy for you."

"I don't..." he stopped the scratch the back of his neck. "I don't know the songs as well as you do."

She rolled her eyes. "You'll figure it out. You probably know them better than you think. But if you get really stuck, just lip sync. Nobody will notice."

His eyes widened. "*Everyone* will notice. You don't exactly blend in when you sing."

"Awww," Cass said, her mouth curling into a smile. "That's the nicest thing you've ever said to me."

He lifted an eyebrow at her. "Ever?" He'd said plenty of nice things to her over the three years that they'd dated.

"Well, in the last few months," she said nonchalantly. She patted him on the shoulder and got up from the bench. "I really should go before Mom and Dad get home and find us like this. See you tomorrow?"

"Yup," he said, but inside he was twisted up. Cass didn't seem to hate him anymore, but she'd made it clear there was no longer anything between them. And that hurt more than he wanted to admit.

"Okay, dress me nicely, please," she said as she headed for the doorway.

"You, too," he said. "Oh, but not too nicely. Not like...funeral nice."

"Yeah, yeah," she said, waving a hand at him. "Business casual. I got it."

Cass left Ian in her basement and whisked out of the house before he could ask her any more questions. She didn't have the time or patience to get into all that with him—again. Why now? Why couldn't they just focus on the problem they were having and just...never bring up the past ever again?

Her only comfort was knowing that Ian could sing, *really* sing just as well as she could. It should have bothered her, but actually it was a good thing. At least according to Colin and Jess. She just had to hope and pray that if they could pull off the game and the audition on Tuesday, then they would switch back and never speak of this.

CHAPTER FOURTEEN

Cass woke up with a start. Ian's alarm had gone off but it was far earlier than she needed to get up on a Sunday. And in fact, since Ian didn't have to go to church early like she always did, she had the pleasure of rolling over and sleeping for another hour.

Except, she couldn't sleep. Her thoughts were a complicated mess of being Ian and being herself and not knowing where the line between her and him started or ended. Not to mention that Ian clearly wanted to talk about the past and she wanted anything but that. Maybe she *should* go to church early.

She showered quickly, wondering how long she'd be stuck with Ian's stupid, gorgeous body while he was in her...out of shape one. She rolled her eyes. She still couldn't believe he'd said that to her. Didn't he know she cared more about keeping her vocal cords in shape than her muscles?

The longer she thought about it, the crankier she got. Emma seemed to notice, darting quick looks at her as she jammed a fork into her eggs. Cass knew she wasn't making a good impression for Ian, but she didn't care. She didn't want to be happy-go-lucky Ian anymore.

When they got to church, Cass went over to the pews where the youth usually sat and slumped down next Colin who was already sitting with Jess. The choir had finished rehearsing and Ian was casually carrying on a conversation with 76-year-old May, her favourite choir lady. They were laughing at something, which just made Cass scowl even more. How dare he take that from her?

Colin leaned towards her and whispered, "What's up with you?"

"What do you think?" she hissed under her breath.

He put his hands up in surrender. "Okay, forget I asked."

Up on the platform where the choir was seated, Ian's eyes sought and found Cass's. He smiled at her but she just frowned at him. What he'd done now, he didn't know. But trying to figure Cass out was just as annoying as having to laugh off May's backhanded compliments.

So far she'd told him that the pink sweater he'd chosen would have been "lovely" in a deep mauve, had offered to share her music with him because she'd marked hers "correctly," and had told him that maybe Cass and Ian could try one more time if only she'd smile a little more at him. He hadn't agreed with any of the statements, but hadn't outwardly disagreed with her.

"Oh, by the way dear," May said, patting him on the arm, "your F sharp was a little flat in 'Heaven Came Down.'"

Ian clamped his mouth shut in a tight smile before he blurted out how he'd like to flatten her. No sense in arguing with her—he didn't know which note was the F sharp, and he was pretty sure he'd sung every note as perfectly as Cass would have.

He glanced back quickly at Cass and cringed when he saw her talking to Rhea. She was a notorious flirt and ever since he and Cass had broken up, she'd taken every opportunity to try to engage him. He wasn't interested in her, had never been, and had never encouraged her. But now Cass was smiling at her and that was all Rhea needed to even *think* something might be there.

Great, that would be another thing he'd have to explain to her later. He crossed his arms but at that moment, the choir director lifted her hands to get them all to stand. Ian dutifully followed suit, watching as the congregation stood as well.

As they began their first hymn, Ian glanced at May from under his eyelashes. Her back was straight, mouth wide open to dramatically enunciate every vowel. She thought he was singing off-key? Well maybe no one would hear her over his singing. He raised his voice a little louder and, with some satisfaction, noticed her giving him a curious stare. But she didn't stop singing.

Smugly, he looked back out into the crowd and sang just the tiniest bit louder. His eyes instinctively sought out Cass and to his horror he found her singing along. Ian didn't sing in church, like ever. People would definitely think something weird was going on. What was she thinking?

He tried to convey to her what a grave error she was making by widening his eyes at her, but then...*then* she closed hers and he could tell she was really getting into it. Interrupting his singing momentarily to swallow hard, he closed his eyes and sent up a quick prayer.

Thankfully, a moment later Colin elbowed Cass hard and she was broken out of her trance. A little pink coloured her cheeks and she shut her mouth and looked up at Ian. But he felt bad now because her eyes were sad. Sad that she wasn't allowed to sing her little heart out like she normally would have.

Ugh. This whole situation was so frustrating and confusing for him. Nothing seemed to be working out, and the harder they tried to be like each other, the more unhappy they both became. Was it really worth it—to be so much like each other that they both lost themselves in the process? And what if none of this helped them to switch back? What then?

After the singing was over and the choir dismissed, Ian slunk off the platform and plopped himself down in the empty space next to Jess. No less than three curious glances were thrown his way, but he crossed his arms and ignored them.

When the pastor started preaching, Ian glared down at his hands, tightly clasped together in his lap. He didn't feel like being lectured today, but when he heard the words, "'For I know the plans I have for you,'" he looked back up.

"'Plans to prosper you and not to harm you,'" the pastor read out of his bible. "'Plans to give you hope and a future.'"

Ian looked back down at his lap. *Was this your plan me, God? Seems like a strange thing to do...*

He glanced past Jess and Colin to see that Cass was peeking at him out of the corner of her eye. Was she thinking the same thing? Was there some bigger plan going on that neither of them had agreed to?

He slumped a little farther down into his seat and waited for the sermon to be over. It wasn't that he didn't care or was trying to be disrespectful, but today, in Cass's body, he just wasn't feeling it.

God, how much longer do we have to put up with this? he prayed silently.

When the congregation was dismissed, Ian rose sullenly and filtered out with the rest of the youth. He knew the girls normally liked to clump together so they could gossip or whatever it was they did, and the guys would go and goof off somewhere. But today, he chose to go to the kitchen and offer the welcome ladies some help with setting out the coffee and other refreshments.

"Oh, another young helper," Mrs. Abernethy said, smiling right into his eyes.

"What?" he said just before noticing his own tall frame in the corner of the kitchen. Cass was picking up a plate of cookies in each hand. Of course she'd think of his idea first. She smiled at him and he couldn't help smiling back, even as twisted up as he felt inside.

"Here, Cass," she said, "you can take these."

He forced his legs to go closer and took the platters from her hands. But she didn't let go immediately.

"Are you okay?" she asked softly in his low, deep voice.

He shrugged. "Sort of, but not really," he answered, matching her tone.

She nodded and finally let go of the plates. Within a few minutes they'd helped to set everything out in the foyer. But they both retreated to the kitchen again, grateful to be alone for a minute.

"Cass," Ian said, lifting his hand to her face. "I kind of wish you had shaved before church." It wasn't what he'd wanted to say, but it was neutral ground. Or so he'd thought.

She tilted her head and her gaze travelled down to his legs past the skirt he'd put on. Lifting an eyebrow, she said, "You're one to talk."

His eyes widened at the mere idea of shaving her legs. "Oh, I'm not doing that. No one notices anyway."

Cass scoffed and put her hand on her hip. "Uh, yes, people do notice and I'd appreciate if you'd shave before my audition."

He shook his head. "I'll just wear pants."

"But...but," she sputtered. "I had the perfect outfit picked out."

He rolled his eyes. "I'm not doing that. I'll probably just cut up your legs. A face is way easier, so just do your face before the game, please."

"Why?" she asked. "Because your parents think the scouts care more about how clean the players are rather than how well they play?"

Ian's face fell. "What?"

"Your parents definitely care way more about the way you look than the way you play," she said, her tone gentle. "Have you never noticed?"

He looked away, shifting from foot to foot. "This isn't about them," he said quietly. "Would you do it for me?"

She sighed and shook her head a little. "Why don't we...?" Another sigh. "Why don't we help each other out? I'd rather not have cut legs. Or a cut-up face."

He nodded, even though that sounded like a totally awkward proposition. "That's fair."

"Tomorrow night?" she said.

"Yeah, that'll work," he answered. "Umm..."

He'd wanted to say more, something meaningful to her, but they were cut off by voices coming into the kitchen. Ian immediately went to the sink and turned on the tap like he was washing his hands while Cass scooted past him.

Of all the things he could have brought up, he had to complain about shaving. She'd noticed his legs today, but she wasn't actually going to say anything about it. And now there was another layer to this crazy, complicated mess they were stuck with. Ugh.

She rubbed her prickly cheeks. It hadn't even occurred to her to shave and to be honest, she kind of liked the way Ian looked like this. But they'd made a deal. Goodbye, beard.

As soon as she'd reached the lobby, she felt Ian's phone vibrate in her pocket. She pulled it out and found a text from him.

Ian: Practice with me tonight?

It made her smile.

Cass: Of course.

Cass moved through the thinning crowd of people to get to Colin, who had his arm protectively around Jess. Cass had been so happy when Jess had started going to church with them three years ago and today was no different. No matter how weird and tangled up their situation was right now, she was glad to have Jess's friendly smile nearby when she needed it.

"Hey," she said to them.

"How are things?" Colin asked, a little amused glint in his eye.

Cass lowered her voice as far as she could and said, "I need you to help me sneak in tonight so I can help Ian practice."

"Aw, you want me to give away his secret for sneaking in?" Colin asked.

Cass rolled her eyes. "No, I already know all his secrets. What I really need is for you to keep Mom and Dad away so they don't see me playing piano for him."

"So many lies," Colin chastised playfully. He squeezed Jess a little closer to him. "What do you think, Jess? Want to have a little heart-to-heart with my parents?"

She giggled. "I think we could do that."

Cass smiled and put a hand on each of their arms. "Thanks, guys. I really appreciate that."

CHAPTER FIFTEEN

Ian, Jess, and Colin went back to the Jacobses' home after church while Ian wished they could have taken Cass along with them. But that would have seemed weird to her parents considering their breakup. Even though Ian *was* still Colin's best friend.

Oh, the whole thing was just too complicated.

"Hey, Dad," Colin said around a mouthful of food, "Jess and I were wondering if we could have a...a chat."

"A chat about what?" Mrs. Jacobs asked before Mr. Jacobs could open his mouth.

Colin smiled and put his arm around Jess's shoulders. "Well, I'm graduating soon and Jess and I are thinking about our futures..."

"Your futures?" Mr. Jacobs said, his forehead furrowing into deep lines. Ian almost laughed at the overly concerned look on his face.

"Well, that sounds pretty serious," Mrs. Jacobs said, setting her fork down slowly.

Colin cut Ian a quick glance. "Yes...we're *very* serious about it."

"Um, I think I'll go practice," Ian said, rising from the table.

"Okay, Cass," Mrs. Jacobs said, smiling at him briefly. "Now, Colin..."

The rest of her sentence faded as Ian snuck away and quickly pulled out his phone. He texted Cass to come over as quickly as possible and she told him she'd be there soon.

When Cass got the text, she wondered what kind of distraction Colin had managed to pull off so they wouldn't notice her sneaking in. But it didn't matter as long as she could get in and play piano for Ian.

She started to get her shoes on to leave, but Mr. Stokes stopped her to ask, "Hey, buddy, where are you going?"

"Oh, uh," Cass mumbled as her mind went blank. "Think I'm going to get some extra training in."

Mr. Stokes' eyebrows drew in together. "In those clothes?"

Cass looked down at Ian's dress pants and lovely blue dress shirt she'd put on this morning. They looked so nice on his body, but of course Ian would never play soccer in this. Cass chuckled nervously.

"Oh, of course not," she said. "I just wasn't thinking."

She went back upstairs and changed into some track pants and a t-shirt. They didn't look as good as his Sunday best, but...they weren't horrible either. Especially since Ian was prone to wearing tight t-shirts that showed off his muscles.

Get a hold of yourself, Cass. You need to get your own body back.

Thinking quickly, she grabbed Ian's cleats and rushed for the door. She didn't take his car this time, instead opting to jog over to her house. Ian was right about one thing—it was nice to not feel winded by the time she got there. Maybe she *should* consider exercising something other than her vocal cords.

She'd have to think about that later, though. Like after she was back to normal. And then maybe she could take a little run sometime.

Right now, she had to focus on climbing into Colin's room from the tree in the backyard. She knew Colin had done it hundreds of times, and Ian had likely done it quite a few as well. She had the advantage of his height and limber body now. She grabbed on to the lowest branch, flailed around a bit, and finally managed to climb up to the window.

And of course, it wasn't locked. It never was. Why Colin felt the need to leave it open for any eventuality, she had no idea. But right now, she was grateful for his neurotic tendencies. She crept through his room and down the hallway before stalling at the top of the stairs. She had to make it to the basement.

Listening carefully, she could hear Colin and Jess having a conversation with her parents in the living room. In the distance, Ian was doing her vocal warm-ups. Good. If she were quiet enough, she'd be able to get all the way down the stairs without anyone noticing.

She tiptoed down the stairs, avoiding all the creaky spots and finally made it to her precious piano. Ian was sitting on the bench, facing the piano and even he hadn't heard her come down. At least, he didn't seem like he had because he was still singing.

She cleared her throat and Ian nearly jumped off the bench. He whirled around, his eyes wide and one hand pressed against his chest. He let out a sigh of relief when he realized it was her.

"There you are," he whispered. "I've been doing these warm-ups for, like, ten minutes."

She shrugged and tossed him a saucy smile. "I normally warm up for at least fifteen."

"Seriously?" he asked, his eyebrows squished together.

She nodded and came to sit next to him, scooting him over a bit so she could be centred to middle C. "Come on, let's get going before my mom gets suspicious."

Ian nodded mutely and waited for her to play. He let the light, jaunty intro of "Fidelity" wash over him. He liked the song well enough, and Cass was right, it did suit her voice. But every time he sang it, it made him sadder and sadder. Ironically, "Wishing You Were Somehow Here Again" didn't feel nearly as depressing. Plus, Ian kind of liked the way it felt to reach for those high notes and actually hit them. Now he understood why Cass always got so into her singing.

"Knock knock."

They both turned to see Colin in the doorway, smiling at them. "Hey, Mom and Dad are gone. And you guys owe me big time—that was the most awkward conversation I've ever had."

"I won't ask," Ian and Cass at the same time.

Colin's smile grew. "You guys seem like you're getting along."

Ian peeked at Cass from under his lashes only to find her looking at him the same way. Yes, they'd been getting along better than they had in months. Granted, it was hard not to get along with the person that was inhabiting your body.

"Alright, thanks, Colin," Cass said as she turned back to the piano. "We have more practicing to do."

"I can take a hint," Colin said before leaving them alone again.

Once Ian had heard Colin go back up the stairs, he said, "I don't think Colin *can* take a hint. He's always so oblivious."

Cass chuckled. "I know, eh? Always gotta spell everything out to him."

She seemed happy. Maybe now was a good time to talk with her. When she put her hands back on the piano, Ian gently placed one of his own on top of hers. "Cass, if I ask you a question, will you give me an honest answer?"

Cass lowered her hands to her lap and half-turned to him, her expression open and neutral. "Sure."

He swallowed hard, hoping she wouldn't bite his head off. "Why did you break up with me?"

She sighed and stared down at her hands. "We talked about this—"

"No, we *argued* about it," he interjected, trying to keep his voice calm. "We called each other names over it and said mean things because of it. And you were so vague that I still have no idea what I did so wrong. So, now I want a straight answer."

Cass was silent for so long that he was sure she'd run around the issue once again. But then she opened her mouth and whispered, "It was because of Ann."

"Ann?" he said, confused. "The exchange student from London?"

"Yes, Ian," she said in an exasperated tone of voice. "Ann from London, with the swanky accent, and the little nose wrinkle, and the shortest skirts imaginable. Ann, who managed to weasel her way onto the guys' soccer team and into every party in town. With the flawless black hair and high cheekbones. Do you remember now?"

"Of course I remember," he said indignantly. "She also had an awesome right hook."

Cass's eyes narrowed to little slits. "Really, Ian? She had an awesome right hook? Was that really worth sacrificing your relationship for?"

"What do you mean?" he asked, lifting his hands into the air. "It's not like I was into her or anything."

She huffed out a breath and crossed her arms. "You could have fooled me."

"Care to elaborate?" he asked, trying to sound as gentle as possible.

Tears sprang to her eyes and she blinked rapidly to clear them. "Okay... It started with her joining the soccer team and how awesome that was. A girl on the boys' soccer team! Girl power, right?" She twisted her hands together in her lap as she tried to order her thoughts. "And then there were the parties. You were always invited. She was always invited. Oh, but they were senior parties so Cass can't come. Even though Jess went to a whole bunch of them with Colin, who was willing to break some unwritten rule for *his* girlfriend."

"Cass," he cut in, "if you'd wanted to go that badly, I would have taken you."

She shook her head and ignored his statement. "And then Ann joined the choir and you thought it was so cool that she was into something I liked, too. As if Ann was some common ground for us or something."

She clenched her fists, breathing deeply to calm herself. "You know what the real deal breaker was? We were at rehearsal one time and she told someone how you and her were practically dating for how much time you guys spent together. I was right there and she didn't even seem to know that I was your girlfriend. Or maybe she did and that was her way of letting me know that I needed to reconsider my relationship with you."

Ian lifted his hands to his downcast face and shook his head once. "She said that? Cass, I *never* encouraged her or did anything to make her feel like I liked her like that."

"But you obviously never told her you had a girlfriend," she said as a single tear slipped down her cheek.

Ian groaned. "I...I can't remember if I did. But what does that matter? You knew I loved you and not her."

Those words drove a knife right through her heart. "Actions speak louder than words, Ian."

He reached out and covered her fists with his hands. "And what do my actions say to you right now?"

She pulled her hands away to swipe at her moist eyes. "That you want your body back as badly as I do."

He watched her wipe more tears away as he considered her words.

How long had she kept all this from him? Why had she never been more direct and just told him what was bothering her? They could have resolved this; they could have still been together.

But then he remembered that Cass wanted nothing more to do with him, that she wanted to be as far away from him as possible.

"You know," he said softly, "after we broke up, I would have given anything to be *this* close to you. But you're right—now all I want is to be back in my own body and anywhere but on your piano bench."

She swallowed hard as one last tear slipped down, and nodded. "Good. Then I suggest you practice these songs until they're perfect."

She rose and started heading for the stairs and Ian followed her. He grasped her elbow and asked, "Where are you going?"

She pulled her arm away and wouldn't look at him. "I don't know. To train with Colin or something."

There was a tense moment of silence where neither of them moved or said anything. Finally, Ian whispered, "Okay."

He sat back down on the bench and listened to Cass's heavy footsteps take her away from him. Her calling Colin's name. The back door opening and shutting.

Then he wiped away the tears that had been falling since she left, squared his shoulders, and looked down at the piano. He played a few notes until he found the one that he was pretty sure was the first note of "Fidelity." It didn't make him any happier to sing it. But at least it gave him something to do other than chase Cass down to yell at her about how wrong she was about him.

CHAPTER SIXTEEN

Cass burst out of the back door of her house to find Colin raking up grass clippings from two days ago. He always was so slow about getting around to that. "Colin," she said gruffly. "Come train with me."

He scowled at her. "I'm a little busy, Ian. I mean—"

"Ugh!" She threw her hands into the air. "I don't want to be Ian anymore, so I need you to help me play soccer better."

Colin shrugged and tossed more clippings into his paper bag. "You did pretty well yesterday."

"Pretty well isn't good enough," she snipped. Figuring he wasn't going to do anything until the grass was cleared, she leaned over and started helping him. "I need to be excellent so I can get Ian a scholarship and then get my body back."

"Who says getting him a scholarship will switch you back?" he asked nonchalantly as he shoved the yard waste farther down into the bag.

She abruptly dropped the clippings she'd just picked up. "But—but you said you and Jess—"

"Yeah." He finally straightened and gave her his full attention. "I said

Jess played soccer for me and I danced for her and then..."

"And then what?" she asked.

"We didn't suddenly switch back," he answered. He looked away with his eyebrows lowered as if he were trying to remember. "Actually, yeah it wasn't until a little while after. I gave her a hug and something zapped us. So, I'm not sure if it even was the soccer and the dancing."

Cass's jaw dropped. "Well, that's not helpful!"

Colin sighed and put a hand on his hip like Cass normally did. "Remember what we told you? Be nice to each other and do each other's thing?"

"We *have* been doing that," she said, trying her hardest not to sound exasperated. "I even got him to take singing as seriously as I take his soccer playing."

"No, you didn't," he said, and he even had the nerve to laugh a little. "He did that all on his own. But I am glad you're taking the soccer seriously, because Ian really needs a scholarship and he's good enough to get one."

"But—"

"And you need that lead in the musical, right?" he asked. "Well, Ian can get that for you. He sounds almost exactly like you and you were already perfect for that role. So, stop griping, put your cleats on, and let's go practice a bit more, okay?"

Cass let out a gust of air as she let her brother's words sink in. He rarely ever complimented her, or Ian for that matter, so she knew he was being serious. But that still didn't resolve the problem at hand.

"And do you expect me to keep playing for him for the rest of summer?" she asked quietly. "Do you think he'll perform in a musical?"

Colin shook his head, chewing on his bottom lip. "Do you have any other choice?"

"I guess not," she said sadly.

"Then just cross that bridge when you get to it, okay?"

He put his hand on her shoulder and instead of just standing there, she came forward and put her arms around his waist. He patted her back a few times, which actually felt really good.

Finally, she pulled away and smiled at him. "I never thought I'd ever be taller than you," she said.

He grinned. "See? It's not all bad."

She chuckled. "Maybe not."

"Alright, so let's go break your new shoes in," Colin said, shoving down the yard waste bag one more time. "By the way, which of you is paying me back for those?"

"Umm." Cass chuckled. "Let's just see what happens after the game." Colin frowned and pulled his phone out of his pocket. "Alright, I'll get the guys together. You go ho—to Ian's house and get his cleats. We gotta get you sorted out."

"I've already got them," she said.

He smiled at her and she smiled back. So what if she didn't want to be in Ian's body? At least she could appreciate that Colin was a really good friend. And in fact, all of their soccer buddies were good friends, always encouraging Ian and supporting him even when she had played terribly. There was something to be said for that.

* * *

Ian didn't practice for long after Cass left. Instead, he went up to her room, flopped on her bed, and crossed an arm over his eyes. Cass's phone went off a few times, but he ignored it. He wasn't about to start responding to her friends on her behalf when he was feeling so torn over the whole situation.

It was stupid of him to tell her he no longer wanted to be with her.

How had she not seen through his thinly veiled lie?

When Cass's phone started to ring, he sat up and looked at the call display. Sighing, he answered. "Hey, Jess."

"Hi," she said brightly. "How are you?"

He groaned and fell back on the pillows. "How do you think I am?" he answered.

"Alright, I was just checking in," she said. "No need to be snippy."

"You're right, I'm sorry," he said. "What are you doing tonight?"

"I don't know," she said slowly. "I spend a lot of Sunday evenings with Cass and...I can't really do that today. Do you want some company?"

Ian's eyebrows drew in as he thought about it. Maybe Jess could clear some things up for him. "You know, I think I do."

"Great!" she said. "I'll be right over."

Jess wasn't kidding about needing company—it only took her a few minutes to get there and whisk into Cass's room. And Ian was still lying down when she got there.

"Hey," he said sadly.

Jess looked around before gingerly making her way past all the clothes strewn across the floor. "I guess Cass really should pick up a little more often in here, eh?"

"Colin's worse," Ian said, sitting up once more.

"Ugh, tell me about it," she said, plopping down next to him. "When we switched bodies, one of the first things I did was clean up his room."

He wrinkled up his nose and then laughed. "Why?"

She laughed a little, too. "Well, because I was trapped in his body but I didn't have to be trapped in his messy room, too. That, at least, was something I had control over."

Ian looked around. Cass's room was super messy but he had no desire to tidy up. That got him thinking, though. He got up and starting moving things around, lifting up shirts, pants, and skirts so he could see underneath them.

"What are you doing?" Jess asked. "Tell me you're not thinking of cleaning this."

"No," he said, moving aside a stack of books so he could see what was behind it. Just a dust bunny. "I just want my sweater back."

"Ian..." She sighed. "Maybe you shouldn't—"

"It's *my* sweater, Jess," he said, glancing at her quickly. She was still sitting in the same position on Cass's bed. "If Cass doesn't want me anymore she shouldn't get to keep it."

Jess sighed again and then let out a short, breathy laugh. "I can't believe you've been sleeping here the last few nights and never found it."

"Huh?"

He turned towards her in time to see her lean over and pick up Cass's pillow. There, underneath it, was his old grey sweater. The one where he'd worn thumbholes through the cuffs, the one on which the zipper didn't even work anymore.

"What?" Ian said, slowly coming back to the bed. "Why is this...?" He looked into Jess's knowing eyes. "How did you know that was there?" he asked instead of finishing his other question.

"I probably know Cass better than anyone," she said softly. "And I know for sure that she's not quite over you yet."

Heart racing in his chest, he reached out and touched the sweater with his fingertips, but he couldn't bring himself to pick it up.

"Well?" Jess said, tilting her head. "Are you gonna take it or what?"

Ian shook his head, swallowing hard. "It's...it's not like it's going home with me right now anyway. I'll just...leave it for now."

She smiled. "You want to do something fun?"

He cocked an eyebrow at her. "You consider bra shopping fun, so..."

She laughed out loud. "Well, you'll need a new one after we pick out a dress for prom."

His face fell. "Who's taking Cass to prom?" he asked roughly.

Her eyebrows rose to her forehead. "No one," she said softly. "No one's asked her who she's actually interested in."

"Oh."

"*You*," she said, pushing him playfully. "You know you're the only person she cares about."

Ian rolled his eyes, but he couldn't help a little smile. Since Jess had claimed to know Cass better than anyone and she was vouching for her feelings towards him, he had no choice but to trust her—at least a little bit.

"Well, I'm not sure that's totally true," he said, "but I won't be picking out her prom dress. I know how crazy girls are about that stuff."

She smiled. "I was kidding about that anyway. I just thought we could watch a movie or something."

"Oh," he said. "Here?"

"Well...between you and me, the Jacobses have the best sound system," she said.

"Okay, you're absolutely right about that," he answered. Taking one final glance at his ratty sweater, he covered it up once more with Cass's pillow. "Alright, one movie, just you and me. I could do that."

"Yay!" Jess bounced up from the bed, clapping her hands. "I'll even let you pick."

As they made their way out of Cass's bedroom, he said, "You know what, Jess? You're a good friend. You pick the movie."

"Awesome!"

They went down to the living room and Ian made himself cozy on the couch while Jess flipped through whichever movies looked interesting enough for her to watch. Even though the Jacobses' house was like a second home to him, he felt awkward and out of place hanging out in his current condition.

Halfway through the movie, he could hear Cass and Colin's parents come back home. Mrs. Jacobs poked her head into the darkened living room and smiled at them like nothing was amiss.

"Hey, girls," she said. "Oh, *Step Up Revolution*. I love that one!"

"You're welcome to join us," Ian blurted out, knowing that was exactly what Cass would have said.

"Oh, that's very nice of you, sweetie," she said. "But I'll leave you girls alone. Thanks, anyway."

"Bye, Mom," he said without missing a beat.

"You're really getting the hang of this," Jess whispered with a saucy smile.

"Shut up," he muttered, elbowing her while she laughed. His ears caught the unmistakable sound of the front door again, and two sets of boys' feet trudging through the house.

"Hey...?" Colin said from the doorway, one eyebrow high on his forehead. "You guys are...watching a movie together?"

Jess paused the movie and smiled pertly at them. "Like we do almost every Sunday. Get with it, Colin." She glanced past him to Cass, who was awkwardly hanging back. "You can watch with us."

"Okay," Cass said quietly. It only took her a second to realize the only place she could possibly sit was either next to Ian or next to Jess. And Colin was already heading to the spot next to Jess, so...

As soon as she sat next to him, Ian leaned over and whispered, "Does this guy ever wear a shirt in the movie?"

"No, and that's why we like it," she answered under her breath.

Ian smirked but stayed quiet as they watched the last half of the movie. Cass watched Ian out of the corner of her eye, surprised to find he actually seemed really into the movie. And then she thought about how much fun she'd just had playing soccer with Colin and his friends. Oh no—what if they were truly turning into each other?

Cass barely waited for the credits to start rolling before she jumped up from the couch and said, "Okay, well, I guess I should go..."

Ian nodded. "Yeah. See you tomorrow?"

"Yeah," she answered quietly.

"Um, mind if I catch a ride home?" Jess asked.

Cass sighed in relief. At least she didn't have to be alone with Ian's body again just yet. "Yeah, sounds great."

Jess smiled and hugged Colin tightly. "See you later, babe."

"See you," he said, tapping her on the nose. "Cass...be careful, okay?"

"Oh my gosh, Colin," she said, rolling her eyes. "You said yourself that I'm a better driver than Ian is."

"You said that?" Ian asked, his little nose wrinkled up.

"No," Colin said while Cass said, "Yes."

"Come on," Jess said, taking Cass's elbow. "I can't stay here forever."

Cass led Jess out to Ian's car. It was a short ride, but she still made sure to drive as carefully as she'd been taught to.

"So..." Jess broke the silence. "How does it feel to have your own car?"

Cass actually laughed. "Not gonna lie, it's kind of nice. Definitely not the worst part about being in Ian's body."

"Mmmhmm," Jess mused. "And what's the best part about it?"

Cass thought honestly about the question and finally answered, "Going running with my brother without it being weird. Well, at least not too weird."

"Hey," Jess said gently as Cass pulled up to her house. "You know, if you really wanted to go running with Colin, I'm sure he'd be happy to do that. It doesn't have to be awkward."

Cass nodded. "Yeah, you're probably right."

Jess put her hand on Cass's arm. "You're not upset that I watched one of our movies with Ian, are you? He just seemed like he needed some cheering up and you were out with Colin..."

Cass smiled and took Jess's hand. "Jess, you are the best friend anyone could ever have, and that includes Ian. I'm not mad."

Jess smiled. "Tomorrow's a new day. Everything will be okay."

Cass watched her get out and go into her house, hoping and praying that Jess was right about that.

CHAPTER SEVENTEEN

Cass woke up Monday morning with a renewed purpose. Maybe Colin was right—maybe it wasn't about playing soccer like a pro for Ian. Maybe it was just about being nice to him and doing nice things for him, which included playing his game. And maybe there was something else she could do for him, too...

After her morning run with Colin—which she was really starting to enjoy—she picked out some nice clothes to wear. Not too nice but nice enough to look...

Really good, she had to admit as she looked in the mirror. Ian had always looked good in blues and greens, which brought out the blue in his eyes and the pink in his cheeks. So she put him a checkered shirt and dark wash jeans, and then styled his hair the way she'd always liked.

She gave her reflection a smile, the same smile that had always managed to make her heart beat double time. Today was no different but this wasn't about her right now.

She picked Colin up once more and thankfully he was silent about her driving this time. She was surprised to find Ian and Jess had gotten there before them. But even more surprising was the way Ian looked.

He had dressed her in a gorgeous mauve blouse that she hadn't worn in a while. It was a shirt he had bought for her birthday last year and even though she adored it, she hadn't been able to wear it since their breakup. But obviously he liked it just as much as she did. On top of that, his makeup was flawless and she guessed she had Jess to thank for that.

"Wow," she breathed, stopping a few feet away from him. "You look so good today."

Ian's cheeks flushed a little under her gaze. "Well, you look...you look really great, too. I didn't even remember that shirt existed."

Cass blushed in response, too, and they both stood there awkwardly. Finally, she opened her mouth to say more, but the bell rang. "See you tonight?" she asked quietly while the other students rushed around them.

"Yeah," he answered, a little smile on his face.

She was too distracted to really focus on Ian's classes. She did feel a little bad about that, but she was still hoping she wouldn't have to finish the school year as him.

Focus, Cass.

Third period had just finished and she had to rush to get to the other side of school where Christy's locker was. She rounded the corner, took a deep breath to make it look like she hadn't just been running, and raked her fingers through her hair to give it that carefully disheveled look that she loved so much.

Er, no, that she *used* to love. She didn't love it anymore; she just hoped Christy did.

"Hey," Cass said as she leaned against the locker next to Christy's. Christy turned to her abruptly, her face breaking out in a wide smile. Cass gave her Ian's heart-stopping smile. "How's it going?"

"I'm good," Christy said. She glanced up and down at the shirt Cass had put on. "What's up?"

Cass shrugged. "I heard you didn't have a date for the prom. And, uh...I don't have one, either. So, how 'bout it? You wanna go with me?"

Christy's eyes flashed with attraction while a little part of Cass died inside. But as Christy's smile began to fade, Cass felt something else—disappointment? Confusion? Regret?

"Wow, Ian, that's so nice of you to ask," Christy said.

"Alright," Cass said, giving her that special smile again. "So, just tell me what colour your dress is and I'll pick you up at, say, 6:30?"

Christy hesitated. "Um...no, Ian," she said gently.

"6:45?" Cass asked hopefully.

Christy laughed but Cass could tell it was forced. "Listen, I'm really flattered, but I think I'm gonna have to say no."

Cass swallowed hard. Christy was saying no to Ian even though she seemed super into him? "Why?" she asked, not caring whether or not that's something Ian would have said.

Christy's pretty brown eyes flashed with a touch of disappointment. "Look, you're a really great guy and honestly, you look hot today. But...I don't really want to go to prom with someone who's going to be thinking about another girl all night long."

"Wait...what?" Cass asked, her brows knitting together. "What do you mean?"

Christy sighed and turned to her locker to pull a book out. "I mean Cass, obviously."

"What about her?" Cass asked, forcing her voice to remain neutral. "We broke up months ago."

"Yeah, well..." Christy shut her locker and wouldn't quite look into Cass's eyes. "I mean, I saw the way you were looking at her in church yesterday. And earlier today...I heard you tell her she looked good." She shrugged but Cass could tell she was crushed.

"Oh, that's...that's really *not* what it looked like," Cass said, putting her hands up. "I swear. It's hard to explain but—"

"It's not that hard. You're still into her." Christy finally met her eyes and smiled gently. "It's okay. I'm going with my gals anyway. Maybe we can have a dance together, but not the whole night. Okay, Ian?"

Cass swallowed hard. Great, she had screwed this up for Ian without even knowing it. She hoped he wouldn't be too mad. "Okay, Christy. Thanks anyway."

Christy turned, threw a "goodbye" over her shoulder, and then walked away, leaving Cass more confused than ever. She hadn't expected Christy to say no to her, especially not for the reason she gave.

The bell rang again, and Cass grunted before taking off for Ian's next class. She was late and the teacher waved her in impatiently before handing her a pop quiz. Great. Another thing she would mess up for Ian. She *had* to do well at that game tomorrow.

At the end of the day, instead of going to the locker room to change, she went to Jess's locker. Jess raised an eyebrow at her and looked around at the other students before greeting her.

"What's up?" Jess asked quietly.

Cass looked around, too and when she was sure no one would be listening, she whispered, "I ask Christy to go to prom with—with Ian."

Jess's eyes widened and she said a little louder, "*Really*? What possessed you to do that?"

Cass motioned down at Ian's body. "I knew he was interested and she seemed plenty interested, too. I was trying to do the right thing, to do something for Ian that had nothing to do with my own desires."

"Your own desires?" Jess repeated, her eyes lighting with amusement. Cass rolled her eyes.

"Okay, so what... Are you stuck with a beautiful prom date now?" Jess asked.

"No," Cass said, shaking her head slowly. "Can you believe it? She said no to *this*." She gestured down at herself. "To Ian Stokes. Do you know how many girls want to go to prom with Ian?"

Jess smirked. "I can think of at least one."

"*Jess*." Cass sighed. "I feel like I seriously messed up."

Jess shrugged. "What's done is done now. Don't you have a practice to get to?"

"Ugh, yes." She shook her head. "Okay, I'll see you later. Thanks, bestie."

"Anytime, dude," Jess said with a wink.

*   *   *

Ian had intended to watch the soccer team practice after school ended, but the choir director, Mrs. Dean, caught him as he was headed towards the back doors.

"Hey, Cass," she said in her pleasant, sing-song voice. "The quiet room is all yours now."

"Um, what?" he blurted out without thinking.

Mrs. Dean tilted her head at him. "Didn't you say you would like to practice there before your big audition tomorrow?"

Ian hesitated. Cass hadn't mentioned it but maybe she'd just forgotten? They'd both been so focused on other things. Now that he thought about it, it did sound like a good idea. He smiled. "Oh yeah, I almost forget. Thanks, I'll head right there!"

He turned around and started walking. To where, he had no idea. Cass would know but she had to have been getting ready to play by now. He texted Jess, who told him it was inside the choir room.

Duh. Of course it is, Ian.

The small, padded room only had two chairs and one music stand in it. Ian didn't need either. Instead, he got out Cass's phone, plugged in her headphones, and played her music. He'd discovered without her help that reaching the highest notes in her songs was easier while standing, so he ignored the chairs and belted out the songs.

He didn't stay long, though. The more he practiced and thought about Cass's audition tomorrow, the more his stomach twisted up into knots. Here in the quiet room and sitting on Cass's piano bench with her next to him, he felt totally confident. But he wasn't sure how he would do singing in front of people he didn't know, who would be judging him solely on something he'd only learned to do a few days ago.

Though he hadn't practiced for very long, by the time he'd finished he felt a tickle in his throat. One he wasn't entirely comfortable with. Oh no! He couldn't be getting sick. No, there was no way.

As soon as Mrs. Jacobs came home from work, he immediately said to her, "Mom, I need some more of the stuff."

Mrs. Jacobs lifted an eyebrow as she slung her purse off her shoulder. "What stuff?"

"The stuff for my throat," he said, verging on hysteria. Maybe it was just the nerves getting to him. "It's starting to feel scratchy."

"Oh, sweetheart." Mrs. Jacobs reached out and cupped his cheek. "You always get like this before an audition."

He did? Or rather—Cass did? He put a hand up to his throat and grimaced. This was an awful feeling.

"I'll make you some of your lemon water," Mrs. Jacobs said gently as she moved through the house. "But really, you just need to relax and not get all tensed up. That's what makes it worse, remember?"

"You're right," he said. It was true for any discipline, really. He knew he couldn't play soccer if he was too tense, and the same was true for singing. He would just have to calm down and trust in Cass's voice to get him through tomorrow.

Mrs. Jacobs brought him some of that gross-tasting stuff she'd given him a few days prior. "Thank you," he said. He knew it would taste awful, but he truly was grateful for her support, even if for Cass's sake.

Even though he still couldn't quite keep the gag reflex down, he drank the whole cup of "special water." Cass would thank him later, he was sure. Speaking of later...

He looked down at his legs, even though he'd put on jeans today. He couldn't see the hairs that had been steadily growing since they had switched bodies, but she could certainly feel them. And they were more uncomfortable than he thought they'd be. All he could do was wait for later tonight when Cass said she'd come over so they could...shave each other.

He shuddered at the weird and awkward thought. And it didn't get any less weird or awkward when Cass snuck into her house long after everyone else had gone to bed that night. She'd brought his razor with her and was passing it back and forth between her hands.

"You know," she said as she led him to the bathroom in the basement, "I could probably do this myself."

"Do you want cuts all over your face?" Ian asked.

"No."

"Then just let me do it."

Ian wet his razor and started towards Cass's face but she pulled back quickly, her eyebrows drawn in tightly. "What, no shaving cream?" she asked.

"No," he said, stilling his hand. "Just trust me, okay? You'll be fine."

She kept her head straight and gaze leveled on him as he made the first shave down her right cheek. It wasn't as bad as she thought it would be.

"Ian," she said, hesitating. "I have to tell you something."

"Can it wait?" He stopped to look into her disappointed eyes. "Only because this won't be easy if you're talking."

"Oh, yeah, of course," she said, before clamping her mouth shut.

"Relax your face, I'm almost done," he said.

Chills ran down her spine as Ian's breath touched her freshly shaved face. She shifted uncomfortably, which caused Ian to nick her in the chin.

"*Ow.*"

"Well, why'd you move like that?" he asked, scowling at her. He quickly grabbed some toilet paper and dabbed at her chin with it.

"I don't know," she said, frowning at him, too. "This body is so…unpredictable."

His frown disappeared and he nodded like that made any sense to him. "Well, it's not a bad cut. Hey, you want just a mustache?"

She laughed out loud. "Ew, no. That wouldn't look good on you."

He smiled. "Okay, just hold very still now. I'm almost done."

A few quick swipes above her lip and then Ian stepped back to run the razor under the tap. Cass smiled into her reflection, turning her face left and right and running her fingers down his cheeks.

"Wow. You know, if I don't do well tomorrow, you could just become a barber," she joked. She looked down at his bare legs, the short shorts he'd put on. "Your turn."

"How should I…?" He spread his legs apart and his hands up.

"Yeah, just put your leg up on the toilet," she told him as she got out her can of shaving cream.

As she applied the wet cream to his leg, he asked, "What did you want to tell me?"

"Oh." She dreaded telling him about how she'd messed up earlier today but he deserved to know. "I, uh…I asked Christy to the prom today."

Ian's eyebrows rose but he didn't look angry. "You did?"

Cass nodded and started shaving his leg, carefully pulling the razor down in a motion that was familiar to her yet strange all the same. She stayed silent for several minutes as she made her way around the leg.

"Um, so...what did she say?" he asked patiently.

She turned to rinse off the razor before answering. "She said no. I'm sorry, Ian." Finally, she looked him in the eye. "I wish..."

He shrugged. "Don't be sorry. It's not your fault she didn't want to go with me."

"Um, well, it kind of is."

"How so?"

"Can you straighten your leg?" She waited for him to put his foot down and straighten out so she could shave the front and back of his knee. "She...she didn't want to go because she thinks you're still into me."

Ian didn't say anything at first so Cass wiped down his leg and started on the other one. Just when she'd started, he said quietly, "She's not like...one hundred percent wrong."

"So, what like eighty, ninety percent maybe?" she said, instead of addressing what he'd actually meant. Now was just not the time.

He let out a breathy laugh. "That's a little closer."

Cass finished up that leg and then wiped it down, too. When she was done, he said, "You know...you girls don't have to do this. Guys don't really notice that much."

"It's not for you," she snipped. Leaning forward, she touched his calf. "It's for the silky-smooth feeling."

He grabbed her hand and pulled it off of his leg. "Cass... Don't touch me like that. Please."

Cass's eyebrows drew together as she tried to sort through her confusion. "Ian, I was just—"

"I know," he said, cutting her off. "Come on, let's get some rest now.

I'll see you tomorrow."

He left the bathroom without even waiting for a response while Cass floundered around for answers to questions she didn't dare speak aloud.

CHAPTER EIGHTEEN

Despite Ian telling her that they needed to get some good rest, Cass had a difficult time sleeping that night. She wasn't just worried about Ian's soccer or her audition. She was worried about what would happen after.

What if she got a great scholarship for Ian? What if he got the lead in the musical? That sounded great...if they were in their own bodies. But there was no guarantee they'd get back.

By the time she had to get up, she was cranky and exhausted. But she was also determined to see this thing through, so she met Colin for their early-morning run. He was silent beside her like he usually was, but he kept glancing in her direction.

Finally, they slowed down to do some stretches by the park near their house. Colin gave her one more weird look, at which she asked, "What? Why do you keep looking at me like that?"

"Are you doing okay?" he asked gently. "Do you feel ready?"

She'd been about to open her mouth and lie that she was fine. But then she changed her mind and said, "Not really. I think I could play a good game, but I'm not sure how well I'll impress the scouts."

"Is that all you're worried about?" he asked as he leaned down for another stretch.

She shrugged. "I'm not sure we spent enough time breaking in those shoes, but hopefully I won't hurt myself."

Colin straightened and grinned at her. "Cass...do you realize you didn't say anything about Ian or your audition?"

"I—I guess I didn't," she said as she scratched the back of her neck. "But to be honest, I think Ian's going to be totally fine. He...he's a pretty good singer. In my body, anyway."

Colin's smile grew and he slapped her on the back. "You're a good soccer player, too, believe it or not. Look, there are a bunch of scouts who have been watching the team since the season started. I'm sure they already have their eye on Ian, so as long as you play well enough, you don't have to be perfect."

Cass smiled at him and then, because she couldn't help it, she gave him a big hug. "I hope they like how you play, too, Col. You deserve a good scholarship."

"Thanks, Cass," he said. "And you deserve the lead in that musical."

"Aww. Okay, let's stop being so nice now." She chuckled. "Oh! I still need your help sneaking into the audition. It's at four. Please don't forget."

He winked. "I got you covered, little sis."

"Colin, what if..." She stopped and let out a heavy breath. "What if this doesn't work? What if Ian and I are stuck like this?"

He gave her a sympathetic look and shrugged. "Well, then, I'll still be your best friend."

Cass chuckled, though her heart wasn't in it. "Thanks, I guess."

"Hey," he said, putting a hand on her shoulder. "Don't forget you're not alone."

"I know. You've done this before and it worked out for you," she said.

He shook his head. "I meant Ian."

"Oh." She could feel her face flushing with heat as she remembered his reaction to her touching his leg. She still couldn't quite figure out where she'd gone wrong, only that it had bothered him a lot. "Right. Of course."

"Come on," Colin said, already lifting his leg to take off again. "Can't be late for school."

*   *   *

Though he was tired from tossing and turning all night long, Ian dutifully got up when Cass's alarm went off. He was determined to see this thing through, so he got up and started on Cass's vocal warm-ups. They weren't nearly as interesting as the songs he was supposed to audition with today, but he recognized that they were just as important as the drills and warm-ups the soccer team did.

He smiled when Colin banged on his door before shouting, "You sound like a dying ostrich!" He knew he was doing it right.

Colin left shortly after, presumably to go for a run with Cass. That thought made Ian's smile disappear. He felt bad about his poor reaction to the way she'd touched him last night. If Cass only knew how badly he missed her, how much he'd give to be close to her again...

He sighed. He *was* close to her in this twisted, strange way. But that wasn't something they could just fix. The only thing he could do to fix what had gone wrong between him and Cass was to sing his little heart out today. So that was what he'd do.

Getting through Cass's classes was a blur. He couldn't focus on anything and he just hoped he wasn't messing things up for her. There was just too much at stake for them today. He passed Cass once or twice in the hallways between classes. She looked just as nervous as he felt but there wasn't time to stop and talk about it.

He was comforted by Jess, who never left his side as long as she could help it. She didn't say much to him—he was sure she and Cass would have been chatting all day long—but she was there and that was enough.

At the end of the day, he found Jess at her locker and smiled at her. She smiled back and patted him on the shoulder. She probably would have given Cass a full hug, but he wasn't going to ask her for that.

"Is everything alright?" she asked. "Are you all set for your audition?"

He nodded. "I just...wanted to say thank you for putting up with me for the last few days. You've been really nice to me."

"Ian," Jess said in a low voice, "you may not be my best friend in the whole world, but you *are* still my friend. I'm not going to leave you high and dry."

That made his smile grow. "Well, that almost makes me forget that you tried to break me and Cass up on our first date."

Jess laughed. "That was so long ago. And also, I was kind of in an awkward predicament. So...you know..."

"Yeah, I know," he said, laughing, too. How funny to think that at the time, Jess had been in Colin's body and Colin in Jess's and he hadn't even known it.

"Come on," she said, shutting her locker. "Let's go and get you ready for your audition. Cass'll meet you there, right?"

He nodded as they started walking. Back at the Jacobses' house, they once again found themselves in Cass's disaster of a room.

"Lucky for you," Jess said, heading for the closet, "I know what Cass was planning to wear. And it's in here, not getting wrinkled."

She pulled out a knee-length white dress covered in red and pink flowers. It had wide straps and a sweetheart neckline and Ian could already tell it would look amazing on Cass. On him.

"How long has she had that?" he asked as he took it from Jess.

"Umm...a few months," Jess said. "She bought it for a date that never happened." She shrugged and turned around so Ian could change.

As he took his clothes off, he asked, "A date?"

"With you," Jess answered. "Like she's ever looked at anyone but you."

His face heated up but he ignored her comment. "This is an awesome dress," he said, slipping it over his head. Once it was on, he patted down his body to see how it fit and discovered a secret. "Jess, it has pockets!"

Jess whirled around and smiled at the image of Ian with his hands in the pockets of the dress and a grin on his face. "Well, that's the real reason she bought it. Okay, go sit." She pointed to the vanity table.

"She already looks perfect," he said, even as he sat in front of the millions of makeup products.

"Be sure to tell her that," Jess said. "In any case, I'm just gonna add a few little touches, that's all."

Jess went to work on Ian's face and even though he thought it was a little too much, it was still nice. Just when Jess was almost finished they heard a voice at the door.

"Knock knock." It was Colin. "Oh, wow, that's a nice dress."

Ian turned around and stuck his hands in the pockets. "I know, right? It even has pockets."

Colin rolled his eyes. "You sound like a girl."

Ian smirked. "I *am* a girl."

Colin's forehead pinched and he said slowly, "Cass...?"

Ian burst out laughing. "Nope. Just a poor imitation."

Colin tilted his head. "I'd say it's a pretty good one."

Ian blushed and ducked his head. "Stop. Are you ready? I *really* need Cass to be in that audition. There's no way I'm doing it Acapulco."

Colin smacked his forehead and Jess laughed while they both said, "*A capella*."

"Whatever." Ian rolled his eyes. "You knew what I meant."

"Cassidy!" Mrs. Jacobs called from down the stairs. "Are you almost ready, sweetheart? We don't want to be late."

Ian took a deep breath and smoothed out his dress as his friends looked on. "Alright, here I go. Are you guys gonna hug me or what?"

Jess and Colin laughed and both gave him a hug. "Don't worry," Colin said, thumping him on the back. "I'll make sure Cass is there."

Ian headed down to Mrs. Jacobs and together they made their way to the local theatre. Ian was a now a jittery bundle of nerves. He texted Cass several times and she kept responding that everything would be fine. Finally she told him to stop bugging her and just focus on breathing exercises.

Breathing? He was on the verge of hyperventilating and he knew that wouldn't do him any good. He drew a few calming breaths and reminded himself that Cass's vocal cords would do most of the work for him. He just had to remember the lyrics.

Ian and Cass's mom sat in a waiting room full of other girls and boys were waiting for their chance to impress the judges. It was 3:50 and Ian was up next. Where was Cass?

Mrs. Jacobs took her cell phone out of her purse. "Hello?" she said, after lifting it to her ear. "Colin? What's the—? How'd that happen? Oh, well, sweetheart, I can't exactly leave right now... Hang on." She turned to Ian with a disappointed look on her face. "Colin says he has a calf cramp."

"Oh, Mom, you should go and help him," Ian said quickly, nudging her arm a bit.

"Are you sure?" she asked. "You're almost up..."

"It's fine," he said brusquely, glancing at the clock. "Colin needs you more than me right now. I'll just wait for you here until you're done."

"If you say so." She picked her phone back up and with a sigh, said, "Okay, Colin I'm coming... Settle down, it'll be fine." She ended her call and then cupped Ian's cheek. "I'd wish you luck, but you really don't need it. You're going to be wonderful." She kissed Ian's forehead tenderly before getting up.

As soon as her back was turned, Ian furiously texted Cass to get in here. He jiggled his leg up and down, looked over at the doorway, checked the clock. What was taking her so long?

"Cassidy Jacobs?"

Ian shot up as a slender, tall woman's eyes looked around for him. "That's me," he said. "But my accompanist..."

"I'm here!" shouted a voice at the doorway. Cass lumbered in past the other auditioners.

Ian raised an eyebrow at her. She was wearing a ball cap, a hoodie with the hood up, *and* sunglasses. What the heck?

"I'm here," she repeated, taking his elbow and guiding him towards the tall woman. "We're ready."

Ian felt one hundred times better with Cass's gentle, steady hand on his elbow. She took the sunglasses off as they entered the small room. Inside there were two people sitting at the table where the tall woman joined them, an upright piano, and one music stand in the centre of the room. Ian moved the stand out of the way since he'd memorized the music and stood in front of the judges.

As Cass took a seat behind the piano, the tall woman said, "Okay, please look into the camera and state your name, your age, and the two pieces you've chosen to sing today."

Ian nodded and swallowed. He smiled into the camera at the back of the room and said in a clear, confident voice, "My name is Cassidy Jacobs, I'm 17 years old, and today I'll be singing 'Fidelity' by Regina Spektor and 'Wishing You Were Somehow Here Again' from Andrew Lloyd Webber's *Phantom of the Opera*."

He glanced quickly at Cass, who smiled and nodded. He gave her a thumbs up and she started playing the intro to 'Fidelity' for him. As soon as he started singing, he could feel the nerves drain away. With Cass playing by his side and her voice already sounding so beautiful, he couldn't fail.

He only felt a slight misgiving when he finished the song and the judges had absolutely no reaction to the song. They didn't clap, or smile, or hardly even look at him. They just wrote down some notes he couldn't see.

The tall woman looked up and said, "Go ahead with your second piece."

Ian turned towards Cass and she nodded with a huge smile. She started the piece a little slower than he was used to, but he knew he had to trust her and follow the musical cues. The song was so emotional and had so many varying dynamics that Ian almost wished he had something along with him to remind him of what went where.

But instead, he shut his eyes and remembered practicing the song next to Cass on her piano bench. That was where he'd felt safest, where he felt he'd sung his best. And it didn't hurt that he'd gotten to sit so close to her months after their breakup.

With the key change came those high notes, so Ian took Cass's advice and moved his hand in an up and down movement to help him visualize where all those notes were. Finally, after what felt like forever, he hit the last note and decrescendoed softly to the end.

When he opened his eyes, all three judges were staring at him. The man in the middle said, "Wow, that was beautiful. Thank you for coming."

"Thank you," Ian breathed.

"We'll be sending out the cast list on Friday morning," the tall woman said with a small smile on her face. "So keep an eye on your email."

"Awesome," Ian said. "Umm, thanks again."

He glanced over at Cass, who had a smile on her face and tears in her eyes. Once again she took his elbow and guided him out of the room. They left the waiting room where all the others were seated and went out into the empty lobby.

"Ian!" Cass put her arms tightly around him and he gladly returned the hug. As she pulled back, a tear slipped down her cheek.

"Was it good?" he asked timidly. "It's hard to tell when no one claps or cheers for you."

Cass chuckled. "I know, but you did *really* good. Normally the judges don't say anything, let alone tell you you sounded beautiful. That basically means you got a role. You know that, right?"

"Really?" Ian grinned. "Wow. Well...I was a wreck before you showed up. Oh, speaking of showing up, I have no idea when your mom will come back."

"Right." Cass replaced the ball cap and sunglasses and put her hood back over her head.

"Okay, what is this?" Ian gestured to her head, squishing his eyebrows in together.

She shrugged. "You got me all paranoid thinking someone might recognize you here. Anyway...see you at the game?"

"Absolutely," he said. "You're gonna kill it."

"I hope so," she said.

CHAPTER NINETEEN

Cass made a hasty exit before she was overcome with the temptation to hug Ian all over again. She couldn't believe he'd sung so beautifully, so *perfectly*. She felt like even she couldn't have done a better job of that audition. And now she had to play a perfect game for him.

She snuck back to his car, her heart on fire. But her good feelings dissipated as she tried to start the car. She flipped the key several times but knew she couldn't listen to the "rr-rr-rr" of the engine too many times before it flooded.

"What now?" she asked the steering wheel.

Cass: Car won't start.

Ian: Give it a minute, hit the brakes, then try again.

"Boy, I hope that works," she said aloud.

She sat more or less patiently before trying the car again. The game was still an hour and a half away, but the longer the car refused to start, the more anxious she got. What if she had to call Ian's parents? How would she explain what Ian was doing at the theatre, of all places?

Even though hitting the brake felt counterintuitive to her, she tried it anyway. After a second or two, the car finally started and she let out a gush of air in relief.

"Thank you," she said, patting the steering wheel affectionately. She stepped on the gas and ripped out of the parking lot. Then she reminded herself that she couldn't get Ian in trouble for speeding, and she deliberately slowed down to an acceptable speed.

She went to her own house, went inside without knocking, and then followed the sound of Colin complaining in the living room. She poked her head inside and found him practically in tears, holding his leg while their mom rubbed his calf for him.

"Ahem," she said, placing her hands on her hips. They both looked at her in startled surprise. "How are you doing, Colin?"

"Uhhhh..." He sat up slowly on the couch. "I'm starting to feel a little better, now that you're here."

"Oh, Ian," their mom said as she rose quickly. "Maybe you can help him. I really have to get Cass from the theatre."

"No, problem, Mo—Mrs. Jacobs." Cass moved farther inside the room and widened her eyes at Colin. "What's up, buddy?"

"My calf," Colin whined. As soon as they heard their mom go out the front door, Colin got up and shook his hands out. "Ugh, that was the longest half hour of my life. How was the audition?"

Cass's face split into a wide grin. "It was...*amazing*. I think he did even better than I would have done."

"Well, I'm not sure that's true," Colin said, patting her on the shoulder. "But I'm glad it worked out for you."

"Colin, you don't understand," she said as she followed him out the room. "He really gave it his all."

He stopped just before going up the stairs and turned to her. "So, he's not horrible?"

"No," she answered honestly, the admission lifting a heavy burden from her heart. "He's not."

Colin smiled. "Go and get ready for the game. I'll see you there."

He turned to go but she put a hand on his shoulder. "Hey. Thanks for all your help. I really mean it."

"You're my sister," he said over his shoulder. "You know I'd do anything for you."

With that, Colin whipped up the stairs two at a time as though he couldn't stick around after saying something like that. But that was okay with Cass. She knew he'd meant the words and that was all that mattered to her.

She turned to the front door but changed her mind before opening it. Instead, she went up to her bedroom and grabbed Ian's sweater that had been hiding under her pillow since they'd broken up. It was time. After the game, she would give it back to him. Hopefully he'd be able to put it on his own body.

Finally, she went back to Ian's house and made it there just in time for an early dinner. Even though her stomach was twisted up in knots, she made sure to eat a full meal.

"Ian," Mrs. Stokes said as Cass shoved more food into her mouth, "don't forget to do something with your hair before the game."

Cass swallowed hard and touched her hair. Ian's hair always looked perfect no matter what he did with it. And this was a *soccer* game. "I think it's okay like this," she said with a shrug.

Mrs. Stokes sighed. "But don't you want to—"

"Impress the soccer scouts?" Cass filled in for her. "Of course I do. And I will. When I win the game." She ran her fingers through her hair, making it stand up on end, pushed her plate away from herself, and stood up. "I'm going to get ready."

Cass went up to Ian's room and pulled out his cleanest soccer uniform, which she knew he'd been saving for today. 14, Ian's number and consequently her favourite, was in bright white lettering across the back of her shirt. Once she was dressed with everything in place—cup included—she looked in the mirror.

She didn't care what his parents thought, Ian looked great no matter what. She ran her fingers through her hair one more time, making it stick up a little more. Perfect. Now all she had to do was play perfectly.

She went back downstairs to where Ian's family was waiting. Mrs. Stokes tsked at Cass's appearance but she ignored it.

Instead, she turned to Emma and said, "Hey, you're coming, too?"

"It's your big game." Emma shrugged and tried to look nonchalant, but it was obvious how much she liked being included in whatever her big brother was doing.

The short drive over to the school left Cass with no time to think about all the various ways she could mess up Ian's game. She'd almost started going over everything she'd done wrong while practicing when she saw Colin already warming up on the field. He saw her, smiled, and waved.

Cass sat on the grass next to Colin and the rest of their teammates who were stretching and passively ignoring all the nicely dressed scouts in the stands. Seriously, why did they have to dress up for a soccer game? It just made her even more nervous..

"Don't forget to breathe," Colin said next to her.

She looked up into his teasing smile and let out a long huff of air. He was right. She needed to breathe and focus on what she was doing.

"Alright, guys," Coach said, slapping his hands together. "Last game of the season. It doesn't matter if you win or lose, what matters is that you play a good and fair game. Of course, winning doesn't hurt…"

Cass chuckled along with the rest of the guys as she stood up. She knew what the coach hadn't said—losing wasn't a big deal, the scouts just wanted to see how well they played regardless. Still, she hoped she could help the team win for Ian's sake.

Seeing the other team doing the same stretches and chatting with each other just like they were helped to put her mind at ease. They weren't superstars, they were just teenage boys. Just like...like her. She frowned, hoping against all hope that once the game was over she could have her body back.

Colin clapped her on the shoulder. "Hey, everything's going to be alright, okay?"

Cass nodded and drew in a shaky breath. All she had to do was a kick a ball. In the right direction, past a bunch of other guys, and get it between the goalposts. Easy.

She got into position and waited for the play to start. She had a clear view of everyone on the field and tried to mentally remember who was playing which position. Ian's special move had always been to stay behind the defense and then curve around to get a chance at scoring. Cass had to put everything into that move.

As the game progressed, Colin made a good number of amazing passes to her, but every time she went to score she was either blocked or she missed. The goalie had blocked her more than the defense, and that was the most disappointing part for her. By halftime, they were down one to zero, and she felt worse than she ever had. Not to mention she'd just played as hard as she could imagine for forty-five minutes and they still had another forty-five to go.

As she dragged her feet towards their coach, Colin put his hand on her arm and asked, "Are you feeling okay?"

"No," she said under her breath. "We have no points. What am I doing wrong?"

"You're not doing anything wrong," Colin said gently. "This is how soccer goes. It's kind of a slow game for scoring. You know that."

"Ian would have scored by now," she complained.

"Maybe, but he's not playing," he answered. "*You* are. And you're doing great. Just relax, okay?"

Cass nodded, but being told to relax didn't help her one bit. When they reached the rest of their team, Coach started telling them how great they were doing, but how they also needed to pull their socks up if they wanted to get the two points required for winning the game.

She tried to listen but her mind wandered and so did her eyes. She looked up into the stands, scanning the expectant faces for...for hers. And there was Ian, sitting between her mom and Jess. When he saw her, he smiled so big it hurt her. How could he be so nice when she was playing so horribly?

"Stokes?"

Cass turned her attention back to their coach. "Yes, sir?"

He smiled. "I know you've got this. Go get 'em."

Oddly enough, the coach's confidence in Ian's ability was what dragged her out of the pit of despair she'd been digging. If he wasn't mad that she hadn't scored yet and still thought she could, then the least she could do was try her hardest and make them all proud.

With only a minute to spare, the team went back to their positions to start the second half of the game. Cass was determined to score at least one goal. One goal and at least they wouldn't have lost and Ian would look like he knew how to score a goal.

She glanced quickly towards the stands and saw Ian still grinning from ear to ear at her. He had confidence in her. So did Colin, and the coach, and the whole team. She could do this. She could be Ian for forty minutes longer.

The whistle blew and she started running, her heart thumping hard in her chest. All she had to do was get in the right position and wait for one of Colin's expert passes. And...there it was! She slid around the defense she'd been hiding behind and kicked the ball towards the goal. It went wide by a few inches, but she was encouraged to see that that goalie hadn't even gotten close to blocking it.

The next chance she got, she signaled for her teammate to pass closer to the net. Scott kicked exactly where she'd wanted and she raced the other team's defense, getting the ball a second before them. This time, the ball went straight into the centre of the goal while the goalie was still somewhere on the left.

Her team cheered for her and ruffled her hair while she grinned and raised her fists in victory. Now she was glad she hadn't spent too much time on her appearance, because she was sure she looked a mess. That didn't matter though. If she could get one more goal, then they would win and she was sure all of those scouts would be impressed.

Fifteen minutes left of the game and Cass was ready to score again. She raced for the ball but as she went to kick, her foot caught an uneven patch of grass and spun out at an awkward angle. With a cry of pain, she fell and grasped her right ankle tightly. A whistle blew and she squeezed her eyes shut.

"Ian!" several voices called all at once.

"Are you okay?"

"Where does it hurt?"

"Can you finish the game?"

That question made her eyes fly open. She wasn't sure who had asked it but the answer was an emphatic and definite "Yes!"

"Are you *sure*?" Colin asked, giving her an odd look. "It's okay if you can't. No one will be mad if you can't."

She knew he meant well and that he was just looking out for both her and Ian. But there were only a few minutes left on the clock and she *had* to finish. She knew that was what Ian would have done.

"Yes," she repeated, holding her hands out. Colin and another guy helped her to her feet. After testing out her weight on her twisted ankle, she smiled through a grimace and said, "See? I'm fine."

"You're sure?" Coach asked.

"Yeah," she said, nodding. "It's fine. It's just a few minutes."

"Alright, then," Coach said, shaking her shoulder lightly. "Let's get back to it."

They got back into position and as soon as the whistle blew, Cass ran forward, making a concerted effort to hide just how much pain she was in. There were only about two minutes left. Just enough time for one more pass.

As soon as she saw Colin with the ball, she threw her hand out to her right, motioning to a spot that was her only available option. With just the slightest hesitation, Colin kicked. She made a mad dash for the ball and, with an agonizing grunt, kicked the ball with her left foot.

Her follow-through caused her to fall flat on her back, and when she did, she didn't even try to get up. She closed her eyes, even as the crowd started cheering. She didn't even open them as Ian's teammates lifted her up into the air, chanting his name over and over again. She did laugh, though, as she raised victorious fists into the air.

CHAPTER TWENTY

When Cass scored the winning goal, Ian wanted to rush onto the field and give her a huge hug. But he knew that would look super weird, so he hung back with Jess while his parents rushed down to see her. His teammates finally let her down and she limped over to his parents.

He turned to Jess once they were more or less alone. "Did you *see* that?" he asked.

She laughed, her eyes dancing. "*Everyone* saw it. You are officially a super soccer star."

He chuckled and then watched as his mom embraced Cass. "No, I'm not, unfortunately. Cass is."

"Hey." Jess put a light hand on her arm. "Don't give up just yet. Also, check out that lineup of fancy people waiting to talk to Cass."

Ian nodded, acknowledging just how many people were trying to shove their business cards at her. She looked tired and in pain, but she graciously shook each of their hands and accepted their cards. She also seemed to be answering questions on his behalf, and he knew he could trust her to say the right things.

After the scouts had had the chance to talk to her, they moved on to some of the other players, Colin included. Only then did Cass look up at him again. He smiled and waved. She waved back, tried to walk towards him, and then stopped with a pained look on her face.

"Go to her," Jess said, patting his back softly.

He didn't need to be told twice. He rushed down the bleachers and towards her, but by the time he'd reached her, his parents were already whisking her away for a celebratory dinner. And now Cass's parents were calling to him so they could have their own celebration.

Ian waved at Cass, who nodded and them limped away with his family. He took out her phone and texted her.

Ian: See you tonight?

Looking over his shoulder, he saw Cass look down at his phone. A moment later, hers pinged.

Cass: The park at midnight. See you there.

He smiled. It was a date. Sort of. At least he could tell her later how amazing she'd been today. First, he had to get through dinner with Cass's parents, Colin, and Jess. It wasn't that bad. They gushed about Colin's soccer playing and Ian told him that he thought it was the best he'd ever played. If it weren't for Colin, Cass would never have made those two amazing goals.

At one point, while Ian was busy pushing his food around on his plate, Mrs. Jacobs asked if he was feeling unwell. He chalked it up to leftover nerves from the audition, but really he was wondering what to do now that he was still in Cass's body. If today didn't solve their problem, then what would?

* * *

Later that evening, Ian lay on Cass's bed, waiting for everyone else to go to sleep before he got back up. He snuck out and headed for the park, where he found Cass already waiting for him. He stopped short when he realized she was wearing his old grey sweater, staring down at the hands in her lap.

"Hey," he said softly.

She looked up at him and smiled. "Hey."

She patted the space on the bench next to her and he finally stepped forward and sat with her. For several long moments, they just stayed in a comfortable silence.

Cass reached out and took his hand. "You were really great today. I was, like, crying."

Ian, encouraged that she'd taken his hand, smiled. "Me? You should have seen yourself making that final goal in record time! I can't believe you did that. And even after hurting yourself. Are you alright, by the way?"

She nodded. "It hurts a bit, but your parents took me for an x-ray and nothing is broken. Just a little twist."

"Cass..." He touched her cheek gently. "Most guys would have stopped playing in that condition."

"I know," she said. "But...you wouldn't have. And I didn't want to, either. The game was almost done and I just...I wanted to make you look as good as I possibly could. I was hoping—"

He looked down at himself, at the body he didn't belong in. "Yeah. I was, too."

"What now?" she asked in a choked voice.

"Look, Cass, if I have to be stuck in this gorgeous body forever, then I might as well say this." He paused to look into her misty blue eyes. "I still love you. I never stopped loving you. And I miss you like crazy." He swallowed back a sob as a couple of tears slipped out of his eyes. "So, if I'm stuck like this, then there's nobody I'd rather be stuck with than you."

Cass swallowed hard as her own tears fell. She sniffled and said, "You know what? I'm just gonna go for it."

She put her hands on his face and leaned in quickly, putting her lips on his. Or his on hers. At this point, it didn't matter what belonged to whom. Ian put his arms around her, his hands on a back that felt at once both strong and also soft.

Cass moved her hands to his neck, the feel of little hairs tickling her fingertips until she realized that something about that didn't feel quite...wrong. In fact, it felt exactly like she remembered it feeling.

Then both pulled back abruptly, a startling realization hitting them at the same time.

"Cass!" Ian shouted, a wide smile on his handsome, manly face.

"Ian," Cass said in a soft tone as she stroked the short hair at the nape of his neck. "It's really you."

"It's really me," he repeated.

Cass couldn't help herself—she kissed him again, this time fully enjoying the feeling. She pulled away and whispered, "I love you, too, Ian." His smile grew even bigger and he leaned back on the bench, shutting his eyes and putting his hands up to his chest. "I missed you," he said softly.

"Me too," she said.

He cracked one eye open and said, "I was talking to my body."

She rolled her eyes but couldn't help the little bit of laughter. "Well, I missed my body, too."

"And I am definitely not going to miss having boobs," Ian said emphatically.

Cass, though she gratefully put her hands on her own chest, said, "Tell me it's not the worst part of being a girl."

"It is the *absolute* worst part," Ian agreed. Then he turned to her and looked her whole body up and down. "They are pretty nice, though."

"*Ian*," she chided, backhanding him on the stomach.

He laughed. "You know," he said in a more serious tone, "I'm kind of glad that didn't work the first time we kissed."

Cass nodded thoughtfully. She almost still wished it had, but she knew he was right. If it had worked, there were a lot of things she wouldn't have discovered about Ian...or herself. "Me too," she said.

He sighed one more time and then stood up, placing his hands in his back pockets. He pulled his car keys out and said, "And, oh boy, did I miss my baby."

She smiled. "Now *that* I'm a little sad to say goodbye to."

Ian took Cass's hands and pulled her up. "I'll cut you a key," he said.

"*Really?*" she squeaked.

He nodded and then shrugged out of his sweater. "And this is yours."

As she took the sweater, warmth started in her heart and spread all the way to her fingertips. "Ian...you're the best."

Walking hand-in-hand, Ian took Cass home, kissed her goodnight, and then gratefully went to his own house. Though he'd meant what he'd said about being fine living in her body forever, he was never happier to sink into his own bed that night.

Similarly, Cass was elated to be in her own bed, with Ian's sweater securely in her arms. And now it even smelled like him again, which was a bonus. When she woke in the morning, she almost wasn't sure if the previous night had been a dream or not. But then she saw her messy, beautiful room and knew she was home.

She went to Colin's room and knocked forcefully on the door.

"What?" he answered grumpily.

She burst into his room and said, "Let's go running!"

Colin popped one eye open and practically whispered, "Don't you think that would be a little suspicious? Besides, we're supposed to be enjoying our break, remember?"

"Colin." She laughed. "It's me."

He jolted upright. "Cass? For real? But—but when?"

"It was late last night," she said, her eyes shining with excitement.

He shook his head. "I knew I heard Ian sneaking out."

"So, do you want to go for a run or what?" she asked him.

"You really want to go running with me?" he asked. She nodded. "Why?"

She shrugged. "Because...it's good exercise and I kind of liked having that time with you."

Colin rubbed his eyes and then scooted out from under his blanket. "Well, isn't that sweet?" he said half-teasingly. "Alright, let's go."

Cass went to her room and quickly got dressed to go running. By the time Colin was ready to go, she had already stretched and warmed up. It was only once they'd left the house that she realized she had foregone her usual morning vocal warm-ups. But for one day, she could let her voice have a break.

As they ran, Cass quickly discovered what Ian had meant when he said she needed to work out once in a while. Her body was not used to this at all, but that didn't mean she couldn't try now.

Partway through their run, Ian joined them, limping just the slightest bit. He smiled at Cass and silently acknowledged Colin. Neither of them noticed when Colin broke away from them to head down the street where Jess lived.

After a minute, Ian took Cass's hand, never once breaking stride, and kissed it. Today was a good day, and every day after would be good as long as they had each other.

A NOTE FROM THE AUTHOR:

Thank you so much for reading my book! I'm always thrilled to share the characters and stories swirling around in my brain, and it's readers like you that make it all worth it.

If you loved it (or even if you didn't), would you consider leaving a review? Reviews are a great way for authors to know where they went right or wrong with their stories and also helps other readers find their next favourite read.

Also if you enjoyed my writing, check out my other books and my upcoming releases. I promise you won't be disappointed!

—Natasja ♥

OTHER BOOKS BY NATASJA EBY

FROM THE KNOCKOUT GIRL SERIES

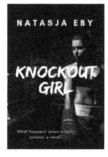 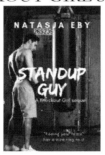

Coming August 2019:

 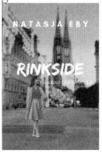

ABOUT THE AUTHOR

Natasja is a librarian and the self-published author of *My Best Friend's Brother/The Summer I Turned Into a Girl* (2012), which was a 2011 National Novel Writing Month winner; *Knockout Girl* (2018); and *Standup Guy* (2019). *My Brother's Best Friend/Learning to Sing Like a Girl* (2019) is her newest release. She is an avid fan and participant of NaNoWriMo and has completed several novels over the past few Novembers.

In 2019, Natasja received two Indie Original Awards for *Knockout Girl*, one for Best Young Adult Novel and the other for Best New Author.

When she's not working on her many unfinished novels, she can be found playing video games with her husband and two kids, singing, or curled up with a good book.

Natasja lives just outside of Toronto—close enough for good shopping and far enough to avoid the traffic.

Follow her on social media!
https://natasjaeby.blogspot.com/
https://www.facebook.com/Natasja.Eby/
https://www.instagram.com/natasjaeby/ @natasjaeby
https://twitter.com/NatasjaEby @natasjaeby

Made in the USA
Middletown, DE
25 July 2019